Metaphorosis

February 2020

Beautifully made speculative fiction

Also from Metaphorosis

<u>Metaphorosis Books</u>

Reading 5X5 x2: Duets
Score – an SFF symphony
Reading 5X5: Readers' Edition
Reading 5X5: Writers' Edition

<u>Metaphorosis Magazine</u>

Metaphorosis: Best of 20xx
Metaphorosis 20xx: The Complete Stories
annual issues, from 2016

Monthly issues

<u>Plant Based Press</u>

Best Vegan Science Fiction & Fantasy
annual issues, from 2016

from B. Morris Allen:
Susurrus
Allenthology: Volume I
Tocsin: and other stories
Start with Stones: collected stories
Metaphorosis: a collection of stories

Metaphorosis

February 2020

edited by
B. Morris Allen

ISSN: 2573-136X (online)
ISBN: 978-1-64076-163-6 (e-book)
ISBN: 978-1-64076-164-3 (paperback)

Metaphorosis
a magazine of speculative fiction
from
Metaphorosis Publishing

Neskowin

February 2020

Pyrrha

Antony Paschos

I open my eyes and see a rifle pointing at me. Well, not at me exactly. At me and Sister. Or just at Sister, I'm not sure, because the barrel is dancing in circles and zigzags. Sister's heavy breathing rumbles, *hur, hur, hur,* lulling me. Her snoring shakes her chest, which, in turn, shakes my head, as it's tucked under her tit. I elbow her hard.

"Sis," I whisper.

She grunts, tightens her arms around me. Then she spots the gun barrel and jumps up.

I can make out only one comrade's face in the candlelight; I think he's called

Yiannis. A lot of people are called Yiannis, not just comrades. Some switched to Yoan or Yanko, because that's what the Bulgarians told them to do. Some refused but when the Bulgarians killed them, their relatives went and carved their new names on their graves.

Sister doesn't talk for a while. I don't know why, maybe because from time to time comrades point their rifles at each other for no apparent reason. Sometimes they even shoot each other, and then the last man standing says that the dead one was an agent. An agent means a bad comrade.

"What do you want?" says Sister.

"Get up, let's go. You, and the girl."

"We're not going anywhere."

"Comrade..."

"I said no! We've discussed this already. We agreed. Perhaps your ears got full of wax and you went deaf, but we've made a deal with the Secretary. So, stick the rifle up your ass and let us sleep."

Yiannis raises his hand to his ear, but stops halfway; he gets hold of the rifle again. "My ears are clean..."

Crackling, the candlewick burns out. Darkness, footsteps, rustling. "Find a match, you asshole, don't you have any matches?" Commotion. I can help. Here. Now everyone can see. My finger is like a vigil lamp, except that the flame is the shape of a dove, quietly perched on my index finger, illuminating the rough walls of the cave, Sister's books, the two logs we have for chairs, the little table with the crooked legs; there's a beach pebble underneath one of them so it doesn't wobble too much.

Clang. Yiannis picks the rifle up from the floor. The barrel is shaking. The comrades take a few steps back, as if they're scared of my little dove. I don't know whether they're really afraid of it, but, truth be told, my doves are often followed by silence. Just like now.

"Shall we?" It's me who asks.

We go down the slope. I wrap my coat around me. The moonlight falls on trails that look like rivers, on pine needle hills that look like giant hedgehogs, on oak trees that look like... I don't know what. Sister would know. Sister always knows; she comes up with the best similes. Not the most pleasing, but the most peculiar. Now, she's holding my hand. Two comrades walk ahead of us, one behind us, Yiannis, with his rifle.

"Are we going to an assembly?" I ask Sister.

"To what?"

"To an assembly."

She extends her hand and touches my shoulder. "My little Pyrrha."

My name is not Pyrrha. I had a different name, once. But Sister gave me this name because, she says, I've got red hair. Same as the comrades change their names, more or less; but Sister says that I'm too young to be a comrade.

Now she squeezes my shoulder.

"I don't want any tricks, comrade," Yiannis with the rifle says from behind.

"Shut up," Sister tells him. "If we were to play any tricks we'd have already burned you alive."

"You want me to burn them, Sis?" I ask. This is a game; I don't mean it. We play this whenever Sister says that we'll burn this and we'll burn that. I don't mind, even though after every game I remind her that I don't want to burn a person ever again. She always says she knows, but I remind her anyway.

"Hmm, maybe later," she replies.

Silence again.

"Sister?" I whisper.

"Yes?"

"Will they give us molasses where we're going?"

"Where did that come from, love?"

"I'd like some molasses now."

"That's what you meant to ask me?"

Sister can tell when I lie.

I pull her sleeve and whisper in her ear: "You remember that I don't want to burn anyone ever again, right, Sis?"

Four more comrades wait for us in the vineyard. I know they're comrades because I recognize one of them. He has all kinds of names, Captain this and Captain that. Some call him Secretary. He wears a pair of pretty riding boots, made of leather, and he's round, with puffed-up cheeks hidden under his beard. Almost all comrades have a beard, but his is thick and frizzy and its hairs look like black thorns.

The Secretary approaches me and squats. He fumbles in his pocket and fishes out something small and wrinkled.

"I don't like gum," I say. I'd ask for some molasses but I dare not. Not yet.

He laughs. "All right, little comrade. Will you show me your magic tricks? And I'll give you whatever you want."

"I'm not a comrade yet," I reply, squeezing Sister's hand.

"You think this is a freak show?" she asks the Secretary.

"Comrade," the Secretary says, gets up and shoves the gum back in his pocket. "If she's going to be a part of this Revolution…"

"She shouldn't! She's a fucking child!"

"Yet if what they say she can do is true…"

"It doesn't matter if it's true! Even if you make her do it, have you thought of what will happen afterwards? What will the Bulgarians do in retaliation? They'll lay waste to the entire countryside."

"Let them lay waste to it, then. If that's what it takes for the people to wake up, let them do it. These lazy-ass yokels put up with anything the Bulgarians do to them; they won't take to the mountains, if no blood is spilled."

"We're not talking about a little blood. There will be a bloodbath." Sister looks ready to catch fire, same as I can set anything I want alight.

"Comrade, we made a decision in the assembly. Do you dissent from the assembly's decision?"

"The decision didn't involve her, did it?"

I don't want them to fight. As Sister would've said, I've had enough.

I light up five little doves, one for every finger. Wings of fire come to life, making the smallest of sounds, *phoop, phoop, phoop, phoop, phoop.* Suddenly, I hear proper fluttering: something jerks up from the vineyard and flies into the sky. I wish it were a dove too, but it's probably an owl, and an owl is never a good omen.

Yiannis with the rifle brings his hand to his chest and makes a quick gesture as if he's crossing himself. The Secretary shoots an angry look at him and Yiannis squeezes his hand into a fist, brings it to his mouth and coughs. It's not that it's forbidden to make the sign of the cross, but the comrades never do that.

Meanwhile, five doves burn quietly on my fingers and Sister has taken her hand from mine and has placed it on her forehead. She mumbles something I can't hear, but I know her and I can read her lips under the light of my little fires. "Fuck, no," that's what she said. I guess I did something stupid. I put the doves out. No one speaks for a while.

"All right," the Secretary says in the end. "But do these damn birds work, or is it just a trick?"

"They do, they do!" I say.

"Oh, they do, huh? And can you do it from afar, little comrade?"

"She can do nothing!" Sister screams. "She's a child, she's not a part of this bullshit!"

"Comrade," the Secretary says. "It's the only way and you know it."

"You mean to tell me that this bullshit plan of yours depends on some rumors about a magic child? Didn't we have an inside man at the power plant? Why do you need her?"

The Secretary shuts his eyes and snorts. His breath smells of onions. He opens his eyes. "They caught our inside man in the power plant yesterday. His replacement supports the Bulgarian Exarchate. Meanwhile, everyone up on the mountain is waiting for the power to go out. We don't have any other options left, comrade. You have to choose, you and the girl both. You're either with the Revolution, or you're against it."

Sister looks at the comrades; at their faces, at their hands, at their rifles. She doesn't answer.

"So," the Secretary says. "Let's go."

The moon has climbed up and the night is now a heavier grey. We walk on unseeded fields. Sister and the seven comrades have swallowed their tongues, as if the animals lurking in the wilderness would overhear their secrets. In the silence, I hear the *hroop-hroop* of their combat boots.

Speaking of boots, the shoes I'm wearing are too big and I've tucked crumpled newspapers at the tips. They're not mine; Sister got them and my coat from a short agent. I asked her whether she'd stolen them, but she said that when we take something from the dead we don't call it stealing. We call it looting. I asked why we call it that and what it has to do with playing the lute and she explained to me that it might be a very old simile, so good that, in the end, it was forgotten and ended up being a word of its own. I'd love it if something like this happened to one of my similes; to be so old that it finally becomes a word. Even though I think that if something like that happened, it would happen to one of Sister's similes. They're very good. Not always kind to the ears, but peculiar.

I walk carefully because my looted shoes sink in the ground, which is dry on top but plump underneath. There's my chance to chat with Sister.

"The ground is like frozen snow," I tell her.

She smiles. She's thinking. Now she's going to say a simile and it's going to be way better than mine.

"Yes, that's pretty much on the spot," she finally says. She couldn't find a good one. "Or like fresh bread, hard on the outside but soft on the inside." She found one, after all.

"Why the long face? You didn't like the simile?"

"It's not that."

"What is it, then?"

"Are we going to start a revolution now?"

"We're going to do shit now."

Sometimes, Sister swears.

I hear someone from behind: "Comrade, what happened to your high morale?"

"Shove it up your ass, asshole."

Sometimes, Sister swears too much. Now the comrades are whispering to each other.

"Comrade, we have to inform the child." A hoarse voice. The Secretary.

"I'll inform her," Sister replies. Inform is a more difficult word to say tell. The comrades use difficult words from time to time, especially when there are many of them around. I've been at an assembly once. I didn't understand a thing, that's how many difficult words they spat out.

Sister informs me. She tells me I must burn the power plant from afar.

"Yes, but I don't want to burn people, OK?" I don't want to burn people ever again. When my doves burn people, they scream.

"You won't burn anyone, my love, don't worry."

"You swear?"

"I swear."

"Do you want me to burn the power plant?"

Sister keeps her eyes shut for a while. She sighs and opens them. Just like the Secretary did earlier on, only that she looks sad and not angry.

"I do. I do."

"And there won't be a bud...a blood..."

"A bloodbath?" Sister asks.

"Yes."

"We don't know that. The Secretary was right. There are times when you have to choose, even if you don't know what."

"All right, then. But, when it's finished, will you find us some molasses?"

"I will. I'll find us some molasses."

I hear a *psst* from behind. A hand stretches towards Sister, holding a small jar without a cap. It's Yiannis. "For the little one," he whispers. Sister looks at him; then, she looks at me. She takes it and gives it to me.

I can't see in the dark, but I can tell from the smell. It's molasses.

The power plant is close to the river and the train station, but you can hear neither the gurgling waters nor the trains. You can hear nothing; not even the comrades breathing. It's a huge building made of bricks. The bricks don't look red under the moonlight—everything looks dark blue under the moonlight—but I know they're reddish-brown; all bricks are reddish-brown.

An owl. It's bad luck when an owl comes to your house. That's why I never light up owls. Also because I don't like them. I like doves. I wish I could make real ones, not just flames shaped like doves.

I lick my lips. My mouth still sticks from the molasses.

A thud. Not close to us, but a couple of Yiannises jump.

"What is it?" I whisper. A second thud.

"It's coming from the trees," Sister says. "Over there, you see?"

She points towards the trees at the train station. Behind them there is an array of train cars and another building, with a roughcast exterior and a round clock on top. A few meters away there's a train car, collapsed to the side, gutted.

I'm not surprised by the thuds; the trees make all kinds of noises. Especially at night, if you're in the woods.

"The aspens stretch their limbs," Sister says. "It's as if they're yawning."

"The aspens are like a fence," I answer and Sister smiles.

"So," the Secretary says—he must be obsessed with the word—"Come on, hurry up."

"What's wrong? Is the Party in a hurry?"

"Comrade, I remind you that when everything is finished I'll have to write a report."

"Who gives a shit?"

The Secretary clears his throat. He speaks to Sis: "Comrade, I'm afraid you haven't chosen a side."

"Of course I have. I just chose the wrong side. The idiots' side."

A comrade makes a move towards Sister—it's not Yiannis, the one who gave me molasses. He holds his rifle with both hands, as if it's a bat. The Secretary places his hand against his chest and stops him.

Sister grants them a glance; then she kneels down and grabs my shoulders. She always has something important to tell me when she does this. Like now. She explains to me what I need to do.

"Do you understand?"

"I do."

"All right," she says and caresses my hair. She knows I like it when she caresses my hair. She likes it too—even though it's cut like a boy's—because it's ginger and soft.

"And then we'll ask the comrade where he found the molasses and we'll go get some more," she says.

"All right," I say and softly push her with my elbow. I hear whispers. I don't light up my doves yet.

"What happened?"

I turn and look at her. "Are there people in the power plant?"

"No."

"And how does it work, then?"

"It's automated, my little Pyrrha."

"What's automated?"

"When something is automated, it means that it runs on its own."

I'd ask her if we're all automated, but, "Hurry up!" the Secretary's yelling through clenched jaws. "Shut up!" says Sister.

"And what are those whispers, then?"

"The comrades, my love." The tone of her voice is the same as before, when she talked about the whole automated thing; flat.

"Sis... You remember that I don't want to burn anyone, right?"

"I remember, love." Here, the same tone again.

"All right." I wait a bit. The owl has stopped crying. Now, I can hear the wind blowing, like a trowel smoothening mortar. This is Sister's simile.

I hear more things, apart from the wind. Whispers: "She's a pain in the ass. Let's just toss a grenade." "The grenade's not enough, you idiot. The machines are inside. Even ten grenades wouldn't be enough." You could say that the whispers too were like a trowel smoothening mortar. "And what's this bitch telling her?" "She's her sister, you asshole." Lies. "Bullshit." Oh, he knows. "Isn't she?" "No, you fucker, the little shit's an orphan." I'm not a little shit, just an orphan. Long story. But Sister said that now she's my sister.

"Love?" Sister's voice; same tone, same tone.

"Yes," I say. And I do what I have to, in order for the trowel to stop smoothening the mortar. That is, to make the whispers stop. Not the wind. Even though, in a short while, I'll make the wind hush too. It happens when you cause a ruckus; softer noises disappear.

I light up ten doves, one for every finger. I feel the air through their fiery claws. It's a nice, night wind, just a bit moist from the stream, but not too much. It swirls around my fingers and tickles my skin where the fingers join.

"Is that it?" someone asks.

A little dove flexes its wings. Another one picks the feathers under its armpit. Or wingpits. Whatever doves have.

Someone spits. "We shouldn't have come. The kid's a fraud."

"Sssh."

Two doves flap their wings and hover above my hands. Another one coos silently. Well, not exactly silently, it makes a subtle *fthup*.

"We'll have to barge in, I'm telling you. And how will we get out?"

"Shut the fuck up!"

"Shut up? With all this bullshit and the damned birds they'll sniff us out. And then…"

My doves take flight. They lift themselves up, more like butterflies and less like real birds, leaving glimmering sparkles as they go—a small flock of flames—and then they enter the power plant through a window on the ground floor.

The fire rises with a gust of wind, *foup*.

"Look," I say to Sister and point at the ground floor windows. "The fire is like a beaded curtain." I look at her, but she's not smiling.

Indeed, orange ribbons dance like paper curtains blown by the wind. My doves are flying inside the building, their wings brushing against wooden beams, chairs, tables, floors, ceilings. I can't see my birds, but the windows, one after another, gain their own ribbons, while a yellow, blinding light pours out of the first ones, the kind of light you can't look directly at because it'll hurt your eyes. The crackling of the fire sounds like a lullaby and still no Bulgarian is on to us. My doves must be sowing fire in the upper floor now, while grey snakes of smoke lash out of a ground floor window, shapes I can't control, with bodies that swell more and more and turn into trees with fiery blossoms. The power plant's burning pretty much as regular houses burn, and as I'm thinking that, over the crackling of the wood and the furniture crashing and the beams falling apart, I hear something. It happens sometimes, to hear something not as loud as the rest of the commotion, maybe because what you pick up is strange or unexpected. Now, for example, this something sounds like fluttering, like an owl's wings, and my heart clenches.

"What's this, asshole?"

"What?"

"Up there."

"Where?"

"There. Top floor, at the window."

For a moment, my heart feels lighter at the thought that the living dove that takes flight might be one of my creations. The next moment I notice its wings burning; it's like the ones I make or, rather, like a firefly—would Sister like this simile? I don't know, I just hear her breathing cut short, and it's strange, my hearing must be excellent to be able to hear her breathing and the bird's fluttering as it manages to fly away. The wind that ruffles its feathers slowly puts the fire out; the bird will make it. It flies off into the night sky. Behind it I hear a hissing sound, something weak and weird that I recognize too. A chick appears on the same window sill. It's tiny and it's frantically looking around and one of its tiny wings is on fire. A small fire springs up behind it; no, it's one of my doves, and I immediately put it out with a small explosion which scares the chick; it hops delicately on the windowsill, slips and jumps off, and I hope it follows the other bird that got away, but no, the chick falls, then flutters and manages to gain some height, only a little, so little. And then I hear the soft thud on the ground.

A hand squeezes my shoulder. It's Sister's. I said that I didn't want to burn anyone; and when I said anyone I meant any people. Sometimes you have to think of every little detail before you say what you want to say.

My doves have faded, the power plant's on fire, but the city remains silent, just like the comrades. Something is moving at the window, perhaps there's a third bird or the flames may be playing tricks, now they look like... I forget what they look like. I hear the scream.

It's a human scream. It comes from inside the building and breaks down into shorter screams, sharp and loud and desperate. A ground floor door collapses and a human shadow appears at the frame in front of an orange, blazing background. It's probably a man. I see him in a blur, because tears have welled up in my eyes since the chick fell.

"The guard."

"Sister," I whisper and feel her moving. Her hand flies off my shoulder. She elbows the comrade next to her. "What are you doing?" he says.

"Don't just look at him, you asshole! Shoot him!"

"Sister…"

"They'll hear us."

And at that moment, they do. Not us, but the power plant, out of which comes a deafening bang that swallows the man's screams. The man runs and falls and gets up again; runs, falls and gets back up. The flames on his body almost fade whenever he stumbles, just like with the birds earlier, but every time he gets up they rekindle, and I don't want to say it, but they do look like wings.

"Can't she put him out?"

The one asking is Yiannis, the comrade who had woken us up, the one who gave me the molasses.

"No, she can't," Sister says. "And now they definitely heard us. So, stop wasting time. Finish him."

Yiannis puts the butt of the rifle on his shoulder.

"Fuck him," the Secretary says. "He's Bulgarian."

"Sister..."

"What is it, love?"

"Sister." I smother a sob. The bang from the explosion has left a constant *iiing* and a buzzing in my ears, as if from a truck engine. "I told you I don't want to kill anyone..."

"Yes, my love, but..."

A shot and Sister collapses in my arms. I step back and her hands fall off my shoulders, they slide down half-clenched, they scratch my clothes and end up on her throat as she crouches on my feet. A spring of blood gushes from her neck, painting her hands, her fingers, the skin between them. A truck's engine. More shots. Voices in Bulgarian. The guard's screams. Yiannis, who gave me molasses, falls down, pretty much like Sister. The Secretary kneels above her. Shakes her. "Tell her! Tell her to save us! To burn them!"

Sister opens her mouth, but says nothing. Shots, fire crackling, explosions, screams. Yiannis moans, injured. The Secretary grabs the rifle.

I drop next to him, on top of Sister, her blood sticks on my fingers, like the molasses on my lips. Her eyelashes flutter. The Secretary aims across the field and shoots—the sound is deafening. Then, a shot from afar, the Secretary jerks away, drops the rifle and falls on his side too. He clutches his shoulder and groans. He grabs my arm with his other hand. His fingers are trembling, his nails dig into my clothes, so I stop shaking Sister.

"Wake up," I tell her, "you swore to me..." I don't want to blame her for swearing to me that I wouldn't have to burn people. Her face is still, her eyes are still, white, like landscapes. "Wake up and I don't care how many of them I burn!"

"Leave her," the Secretary says. "She's gone. Dead."

Sister's blood gathers in a pool around my coat and knees. It's warm and my skirt floats on it, like a water lily. She would love this simile. But she'll never hear another, neither will she come up with one. Perhaps, if I repeat her good similes again and again, then they'll too become words, like "loot" has?

The shots from the comrades are sparse now, but I can hear some far away, from where the truck engine was coming, scattered, then three in a row, three more, two, silence, one, silence. Silence, by which I mean fire crackling and comrades groaning. The guard has fallen silent. Yiannis has fallen silent. Footsteps are approaching, voices in Bulgarian. Shadows in the dark, I can see them moving; they're coming.

"Burn them," the Secretary says, now barely standing on his feet. He's panting, like a hound. "Burn them, they're Bulgarian. Didn't you just say to your Sister you don't care? Burn them, perhaps she's only wounded... Perhaps we can save her, perhaps..."

"Shut the fuck up," I tell him and his mouth drops. It's like an O now. "I'm not stupid and I don't burn people, you asshole." I sound like Sis. I push his hand off my arm. The blood in the pool is now lukewarm against my knees. My skirt is soaked.

"I—I know you're not stupid..." he stutters. "But... But if you don't burn them, they'll kill you."

The Bulgarians are close. Under the dead moonlight I notice helmets, rifles. One of them shouts, but I don't understand a word he says. I don't speak Bulgarian. He must be yelling something at the Secretary.

"So, you have to choose," he says, as if he's talking to himself. Now he's not panting as much. "You're either with the Revolution or against it." And then he gets ready to shoot, but the shooting comes from the Bulgarians. Not one shot; four. The Secretary collapses next to me. There's a hole above his ear, black blood is pouring out. His round belly doesn't seem as swollen now, perhaps because he's lying face down. A black pond forms underneath him, smaller than the one that swallowed my knees, my skirt, the edges of my coat. A small stream of it comes towards me, warm blood mixes with cold.

The Bulgarians are here. They have the butts of their rifles on their shoulders and they tilt their heads to take aim. They say something and they lower their guns. They hang their rifles on their shoulders. One of them takes a pistol out of a leather holder and leans over the comrades. He shoots them on the head. Every bang sounds deafening, but I don't jerk any more, I'm used to it now. In the end, you get used to anything.

I shut my eyes. The shots continue, once in a while, steadily. Bam. Silence. Bam. Silence. I open my eyes. The hand with the pistol is near me. The soldier is skinny and hunched and he smells of garlic and unwashed clothes. His eyes are sad. "Sŭzhalyavam, momiche," he says and I think he says he's sorry. Sister's face seems silver under the moonlight.

The soldier's pistol aims at her head.

I light up ten doves and the soldier steps back. Scared voices, rustling. Rifles pointing at me. A dove lifts its tiny leg from my finger, another one stretches its wings. Silence.

The Secretary said I have to choose. Sister had promised that I wouldn't burn any people. But I did. Sometimes you have to choose yourself. Sometimes, choosing is a total mess.

Every gun barrel is on me. Rifles and the pistol that was aiming at Sister point at me. I wish Sister would wake up and speak to them; if she woke up she'd find a way to save us. But her face is still silver and her blood cold and sometimes you have to choose yourself what to do.

The doves have stretched their wings, ready. But a fluttering that comes from the power plant is quicker. I turn to see and I hear the shot and then something burns my throat and my chest fills with something wet and warm, like Sister's blood around my knees. I see the tops of the aspen trees, far at the train station, the power plant on fire. I don't see my doves, but up there, in the sky, among the stars that blink behind the blurry ribbons of smoke, a bird is fluttering and flies up high; I don't know why, but I'm sure it's the chick that fell off before. My arms and legs are heavy; I can't help it, and I fall like a marionette with its strings cut.

See Antony Paschos's story "Pyrrha" online at Metaphorosis.
If you liked it, leave a comment. Authors love that!
Remember to subscribe to our e-mail updates so you'll know when new stories are posted.

About the story

The story in "Pyrrha" was inspired by the actual events that took place in Drama, Greece in 1941. The blowing up of the power plant by the guerilla fighters triggered a failed revolution that resulted in grave consequences. While researching for my third book, I realized that I'd like to write a story about that particular event. Then, I read a short story about a child that didn't want to grow up, and the voice of

Pyrrha emerged in my head and I decided to give it a try.

A question for the author

Q: Do you have any pets? Do they influence your writing?

A: I used to be a pet to a certain cat for many years – I think she found me too dull a character to write a story about me, though. I grew up with lots of animals, either in our flat (parrots, hamsters, cats) or cottage (dogs and cats). I've actually written a short story about a dog that used to chew on our caravan's wiring, driving my father insane. Now that I think about it, a lot of my stories include pets or animals. In some of them, including a novelette, they're protagonists as well.

About the author

Antony Paschos was born in 1979 and lives in Athens, Greece. He is a member of the Science Fiction Club of Athens. He has worked as a Paintball field operator, a delivery boy, and an air taxi pilot. He currently works as an airline pilot.

Heart of Stone

Chris Cornetto

Light filtered through the debris, igniting a spark in his crystalline heart.

Bending all his will to the effort, the little golem opened his eyes. Pink, hazy dawn — or perhaps twilight? — filtered through a cloud of dust motes. It was barely light at all, yet it set his body thrumming, energy tingling through silicon veins. The light soaked into his heart and filled it with life.

He tried to move his arms, his legs, but he was too weak. He tried to check if he still had limbs, but he couldn't lift his head. Even his thoughts trickled like tar.

How long had his core been dim? Where was he?

From above came scraping and grunting. A rustle of debris, as pebbles tumbled down. More light squeezed through the gap, and the gears of his mind began to turn.

Grand, he thought. *My name is Grand.* He was a Clay, a Stonesinger, a servant of the Lord of Earth. And he had failed his Master.

Somehow, Grand had to make his way home. He wondered if the Master would be surprised to see him after so many centuries — how many had it been? Perhaps the Master would be pleased, if only the smallest bit, to see his wayward Clay return?

It was a queer thought, Grand knew. Emotion was a defect of logic. The Master had no defect.

It was not the first queer thought to have crossed Grand's mind, in his ages in the dark. But now there was light. Unlooked for, unhoped for, undreamed of *light*.

Grand was not his name. The golem had no name, only a designation: GR-A90.

He had taken the name "Grand" on a whim; to pass the years in the dark, he had imagined himself part of the city above his tomb. Through the stone he had felt the vibration of a thousand voices, a thousand souls. He had dreamed that he walked among them, sharing their joys and cares and woes. When they spoke, he spoke back, though none could hear him. His favorite voices became dear friends, and he ached when they were silent.

Grand knew it was mad affectation to play at being a flesh-thing, that he was damaged in ways he could not comprehend. It was his guilty secret and his only joy. It had been a way to pass the centuries.

Then the city vanished, all voices silenced but his own.

He spent another age gently humming to the stones of his prison – a waste of energy, but also a comfort. It was the task for which he was made. He knew the song of every mineral, and with a bare touch could set them singing in purest tones. At his full strength, he could shake mountains.

But sealed away from light, Grand had no strength. He, master of stone, became its slave. It had been a mercy when his core went dim.

The stone above shifted and the pink glow welled through the gap, fainter now. So, it was twilight after all.

From above came a gasp of excitement. A gaunt face peered into the breach, eyes wide with wonder. It belonged to the most ill-fed, ill-favored seraph Grand had ever seen. Even stunted, it towered over him, at least thrice his size.

A seraph. He had never shown a seraph mercy, and had no right to expect any. After untold ages of waiting, his rescue would be his death. The irony stung him.

The seraph shouted in a language Grand could not comprehend, some distant kin of the tongues he remembered. Had the world changed so much in his sleep?

The seraph called out again, turning his back to Grand. No wings. Not a seraph. So what was this flesh-thing?

The golem dredged his recollection, mind sluggish with sleep. Even now, the dim light fading from the sky, his brain threatened to shut back down. He was designed to never forget, but how much damage had he suffered when the city fell atop him?

A human. That's what the flesh-thing was.

Grand had warred with many races, the creations of pretender gods, but humans he barely recalled. They were an aberration, an error, sprung from the dirt with no god to claim them. They had been beneath the Master's notice, and so were beneath his.

A second human appeared, this one bearded, older. Just as gaunt. He eyed Grand skeptically and prodded him with an iron rod, clinking it against his chest.

Grand tried to reach for the bar, but his arms would not obey. He lay in the pit, as still as the rock around him. All he could move was his eyes.

The men jabbered in their strange tongue, until the young one persuaded the elder to help him dig. They pried at the rubble, levering away fragments of broken wall. And, with each stone moved, more debris cascaded down.

The pit grew choked with sand and stone. Grand's small world closed in until it reached no further than his body, more claustrophobic than ever. Panic welled within him. Were they burying him? His thoughts swam with nightmares of eternity beneath the dirt, alone and forgotten.

Anything but that, his mind screamed. Grand prayed feverishly to a Master who could not hear. Let the flesh-things kill him if they must — only, let them do it above the ground, beneath the boundless sky. Outside of this tomb.

Grand fixated on the scrape of iron on stone, the sound of salvation. He *had* to get out. The fear of darkness without end weighed on him physically, crushing him like the very rock that pressed down from above. So close to freedom, it was too much to endure.

Time passed. Grand flickered in and out of consciousness, his power ebbing. Though intoxicating after an age in darkness, his sip of twilight had been scant. Straining to hear the blessed scraping, his thoughts ground to a halt.

Moonlight. Two men in headscarves inspected him, one holding a shovel. They chattered in their nonsense tongue, disagreeing. One enthusiastic, the other annoyed.

Sand and broken stone stretched to the horizon in every direction. The city was gone. He had known it would be, but seeing was different from knowing. It was ironic how he ached for its loss – he who had tried, and failed, to destroy it.

A man placed him gently into a sack, not quite empty. It drew shut, and the darkness returned.

Grand woke to lamplight. He found himself lying on a bench or table. Something made of wood.

Even had he the strength to move, Grand had no power over wood. Its structure was messy and random compared to the beautiful order of stone.

Voices argued. Grand tried to look around, but couldn't. He was sprawled amidst knickknacks and rubbish. He heard the men who had found him bickering with a third.

No, not bickering. Haggling. Haggling over the junk on the table, with which he had shared a sack. They haggled over a brooch, a buckle, an ivory comb. A granite face chiseled off some capital or lintel. The hilt of a long-rusted sword, and so on. All sorts of rubbish.

The men who found Grand were scavengers, which made *him* salvage. He, a Clay, mightiest of the Master's tools, was now junk, pulled from the refuse heap of history.

The shame stung him. An eternity in the dark hadn't extinguished his pride.

Grand lay and he listened, having no other option. Though most of the haul was rubbish, some pieces caught his interest – the gears and springs and tubes of forgotten machines. There were even two small piezo-crystals, which the elder scavenger presented reverently.

The buyer placed a lens on his eye to inspect them. He turned them over in his hand, clucking his tongue as he studied them carefully, facet by facet.

At first Grand thought the collector was checking for damage, but soon realized the man simply enjoyed the sparkle — as if the crystals were nothing more than shiny baubles. He was amazed. How far had civilization fallen? Humans were infants, ignorants. Barely more than beasts.

Grand itched to explain their error, but held his tongue. Even had they shared a common speech, he wouldn't have spoken. With creeping discomfort, he realized that he *feared* the flesh-things. Did they see what he was? Did they know what he had done?

Would they destroy him if they knew he lived?

Perhaps not, but Grand would take no chance.

Once they had settled terms on the rest of the detritus, the younger scavenger hoisted Grand, his large hands wrapped around the golem's trunk. He chattered excitedly about the prize of the collection.

It was an honor to be saved for last, the finest garbage. He was the Lord of Junk.

At least, held upright, Grand could finally look around the room. The walls were lined with cabinets where trash and treasure mingled freely, the shiniest bits of debris given places of honor. Weapons and potsherds and mechanical parts were sorted loosely by theme, but with several wrong guesses. Other bits were unidentifiable even to Grand.

The centerpiece of the whole collection was a golem power core, shimmering and dead. It was too large to belong to a Clay, large even for a Stone. A fissure ran halfway through, rendering it inert.

It was the crystal heart of a living thing. It should have been brought home, to be repaired and born again in a new body. To display it like a sparkly trophy was beyond cruel. It was barbaric.

Grand pictured them prying him like an oyster for the shiny bits inside, and the thought filled him with horror. He strained to draw in light, willing his body to absorb it, but he had no strength to fight. He couldn't even move. He was nothing but a helpless stone doll, who waited centuries in the dark for nothing.

The collector, a stooped man in a gold-threaded kaftan, leaned toward him. He looked weary from the endless dickering, and clearly bored. He rolled his eyes and made an offer.

The young man replied with disgust; the sum had been paltry. The other scavenger gave a derisive grunt, universal to all language. It said, "I told you so."

So Grand was worthless after all. Not even the Lord of Junk. Merely junk.

But then realization set in. The flesh-things were, indeed, clueless. They didn't know what he was, didn't know his danger or his worth. Their ignorance was his salvation. To them, he *was* a stone doll, and nothing more.

Relief washed him like a wave, more refreshing than light itself. He would be a doll until he had his strength back. After that, let it be their turn to fear.

The scavengers finished their business, took their money, and left grumbling under their breath. They brought Grand with them, perhaps hoping for a better price elsewhere. He'd never been so pleased to be stuffed into a sack.

Grand had traded one prison for another, but at least this one had light. Precious light.

His new prison had walls of mud brick and stucco, with windows open to the sky. Outside was a neighborhood of similar houses — whitewashed, flat-roofed, two stories tall. They ran in neat rows along a terraced hillside, beneath an endless blue sky.

The scavengers left Grand in the downstairs room – a living area with a kitchen to one side. A doorway peeked into an adjacent workshop, while stairs led upwards, disappearing into mystery.

Though the living room was spacious, the furnishings were sparse. The scavengers' home felt hollowed-out, full of empty places where things should be. What remained was a table and chairs, some sackcloth bedding, shelves of crockery, resentment, and the lingering embers of faded hope.

The ragged scavengers were father and son. The son had a ragged wife, and together they had a ragged little girl. On the mantle, behind a votive candle, sat a painted wooden soldier, but there was no ragged boy to play with it.

From his perch on the shelf, Grand watched the drama of their lives unfold. Their words meant nothing to him, but their tones, their expressions, told him everything.

Though the old man walked and breathed, he was already dead. He spent his time in the workshop, puttering over junk as if he could restore its lost worth. He avoided his family, even slept in the workshop.

The son was a disappointment to both father and wife, and, by the way he hung his head around them, he knew it. He was a dreamer, always hoping the next haul would restore them to better times. His wife kept him grounded with her scowls.

As for the woman, she was proud and bitter. Though her dress was a rag, the bangles on her wrists were pure silver — Grand could tell by the way they clinked and chimed. She found labor distasteful, and had no words but sharp ones. Sometimes, while the others slept at night, she cried.

And then there was the little girl, skinny and precocious. They called her Farah, and, if there were any smiles in that house, they were for her. Even the old man warmed when she spied upon his work, though he pretended not to see her. Mostly, though, they ignored her.

For want of an audience, she often spoke to Grand, chattering words of longing and wonder, whispering secrets he couldn't comprehend. She showed him her treasures — a ragdoll, a top, some colored glass beads. She had a piece of granite, glittery with mica, that he rather liked.

One time, she draped a garland of wildflowers around his shoulders. Though Grand couldn't fathom the purpose of the dead vegetation, it was the first gift he'd ever received. He wore it with confused and wary gratitude.

Of course, the girl also spoke to the toy soldier, but nervously, and only when no one was looking. Grand wondered if she wasn't a touch daft.

Regardless, she was the closest thing to a spark of light in that dismal house.

After a week of milling about, the scavengers left on another expedition. At last, Grand had a chance to explore the house.

He had prepared for this day by flexing his limbs and testing his joints in his few unwatched moments. Though still feeble from centuries of light deprivation, his body functioned. It was a minor miracle, and he did not take it for granted. In his crystal heart, Grand praised the Master for the genius of his craftsmanship.

Even with the men gone, there remained some difficulties, but Grand had already planned for them. He would make his way down the wall by gently deforming the plaster, gouging a series of handholds. He would do this at night, after the woman retired to her chamber upstairs. He worried that, in the dark, he'd find himself too weak to climb back up, but he'd spent several days basking in the sunlight that trickled through the window. It would have to be enough.

Grand's one obstacle was the little girl. Her bed was a mat beneath the window – one of two mats, actually, though none used the other – where the cool breeze wafted away the heat of the day. Most nights she slept soundly. Yet, if she woke, he would have to...

Grand didn't want to think about it. While it was his duty to return to the Master, his right to kill anything that interfered, he wasn't eager to kill Farah. Her randomness intrigued him. Though she had no Master, she flitted about with enigmatic purpose. She raised questions he hadn't thought to ask.

But, for now, Grand put his questions and worries aside. He scaled the wall, hands and feet boring into pliant stone. He worked slowly, but if caution delayed his homecoming, delayed his punishment, so be it. Perhaps a delay wasn't so bad.

He prayed to the Master that the girl would not wake.

Grand explored the house each night, digesting a room at a time.

First he searched the kitchen, but its barren cupboards held no wonders. He climbed a short way up the chimney until it grew too narrow. He clambered back down and shook off the soot.

Next he chanced the staircase, but only far enough to peer into the room above. Nothing interesting there, either, save a crack in the wall that whistled with each gusty draft. He reached into the plaster and repaired it.

He told himself he was merely testing his powers, that he was irked by the disorder of ill-crafted stonework, and a dozen other lies. The quiet voice inside knew better. He hungered for purpose.

Grand touched the wall, feeling for the Master's gentle pull. Nothing. Perhaps, in his weakness, the straw-laced bricks confused his senses?

The second night, he sneaked outside. Behind the house was a small garden, with a stone corral that ran up the hillside. Though there was room for perhaps a dozen beasts, Grand found only a pair of floppy-eared goats. He patched the walls of their pen, adjusting the stones into a sturdier, more aesthetic configuration. Strength and beauty were inseparable; all that served its purpose well was beautiful.

The open air reminded Grand of escape, of his duty to the Master. At least outside he had solid earth beneath his feet, with no straw to muffle the song of the stones. He pressed his hands to the ground, straining to hear the familiar drone of the Master's voice. Besides the restless shuffling of the village, he found only silence.

Grand pushed harder, flaring energy recklessly. He reached deep into the world around him – and found it shifted, wrong. Barren desert, where rampant jungle once thrived. Mountains thrust up from the ground to twice their old height. The very geography was changed, as if cracked and split and reformed from its parts.

And the voices had changed, too. There were too few, and too many were *human.* Where had the old races gone? Where were *his* people?

Shaken, Grand made his way back to the shelf. Without the Master to guide him, how would he find his way home? What if he *never* did?

It was a lonely thought, but also a relief.

When Grand had failed the Master, he ceased to be useful. He had earned his destruction – it was right that he should be broken down, his parts recycled. Still, if he was centuries late, what mattered another delay?

By the third night, Grand's sense of urgency waned. He would still escape, of course, but in his own good time. In the meanwhile, there was exploring to do.

Mostly, the house was empty and dull, but Grand had saved the best room for last. The workshop was filled with the cast-off fruits of the scavengers' excavations — some neatly shelved, others sorted into piles. He was amazed to find that some of the pieces weren't junk at all, but lovingly restored relics, the tools and toys of a bygone age. There was a signal glass, a mechanical gauntlet, a clockwork beetle, a light-drill, and much more. He studied them with reverence, savoring connection with the world he had lost.

Some of the objects were nearly whole, nearly repaired, with hand-machined parts replacing those missing. Others *were* fixed, and lacked only a power source. The old man was a genius. If only he hadn't sold the piezo-crystals, who knew how many of the devices could have been brought back to life?

On a hunch, Grand searched the room thoroughly. It took an hour to find what he was looking for. In a hidden drawer beneath the workbench, he found two gold coins and a single tarnished crystal.

It was chipped and beyond use to the old man, but not to Grand. The particles wanted to align, to fuse and be whole again. They just needed a nudge.

He worked until dawn to mend it.

All through the next day, Grand bubbled over with impatience. Centuries of waiting, and somehow a single day was torture. But wait he did, and dreamed of the workshop, that temple to the past that was his world.

As always, the woman retreated to her chamber shortly after sundown. Grand pressed a hand to the wall and felt her moving around, oddly busy, but he didn't care. Once upstairs, the woman never came down before sunrise.

The little girl's eyelids fluttered shut, and he was off the shelf in an instant.

Grand scuttled across the floor, as noiselessly as his stony frame allowed. He made a beeline for the workshop, head full of possibilities. All of the tools called to him, but the one little crystal — bathed in a day's worth of sunlight on the windowsill — would have precious little charge for experiments.

He tried not to think how his heart would break if none of them worked.

After a minute's deliberation, Grand settled on the practical choice. Of all the relics, the light-drill would be most useful. With it, there would be no need to blast through the straw-laced bricks – while he could, it would be sloppy, noisy work that might bring down the house. With the drill, he could carve silently through the door when he was ready to escape. When he was ready to go home, and face deconstruction.

As Grand reached for the crystal, he felt the gentle rumble of a key turning in a lock. He froze. The house door creaked open.

In strolled a man with oil in his beard and a swagger in his step. Though Grand had never seen him before, he crossed the house as if he owned it, and climbed the stairs to the private chambers. From above came swift footsteps and a gleeful squeal.

Grand looked around. Nobody had noticed him or thought to look for his absence. The girl was still on her pallet, hopefully asleep despite the noise from above.

There was no telling how long the man would be occupied. Grand crawled back along the floor, inch by painful inch, torn between terror of being caught and missing his chance for escape. What if the scavengers came back tomorrow? What if they found his crystal?

The crystal. It was still on the windowsill. He had to go back for it.

Panic got the better of reason. Grand turned and ran, clay feet clunking across the floor.

He remembered Farah, and skidded to a halt.

Grand peeked at the girl; she rolled over but did not wake. Cursing his stupidity, he scurried briskly through the shadows – not pausing until the precious crystal was tucked safely in the secret drawer. From there he made his way back to the other room, this time with caution, achingly slow.

Upstairs, the animal grunts and moans gave way to silence. Grand felt for his subtle handholds and scaled the wall. He crawled across the shelf and climbed to his feet, resuming his usual position.

Below Grand stood the little girl, peering up at him with wide, curious eyes. She stood on her toes and stretched toward him.

He was discovered, doomed. It was her life or his. Kill her and flee. Reach into the stone and bring the whole house down around them. He would be buried all over again, but he would be safe.

Safe in a tomb.

Grand's mind raced in frantic circles, goaded by fears of death and imprisonment. He was paralyzed.

The little girl poked him and giggled.

For several more days the scavengers did not return, though oily-beard arrived nightly. Farah used the opportunity to make Grand her plaything.

It had been a near thing when she dragged him from the shelf — he wasn't so much lowered as dropped, and had almost crushed her beneath his stony bulk. Though he only reached her waist, he was nearly her match for weight. Next she had lugged him outside and, with more strength than he expected, hoisted him into a little two-wheeled barrow. With it, she hauled him across the little village and beyond, jabbering to him the entire way.

Grand understood not a word, but the sunlight was glorious.

Day after day they came to the same spot, a meadow with a trickling stream on the shady side of the hill. The little village was blocked from view by a spur, but Grand could feel its vibrations, the sounds of life, through the soles of his feet. Aside from the sheep milling in the distance, they had the hillside to themselves.

Along the stream was a profusion of life, a stark shock of color that stood out from the dry grass and, beyond, the dusty countryside. Though Grand himself never knew thirst, he could see the ground was thirsty.

Farah liked to pick the flowers, to talk to Grand and show him her finds. She had a strange ritual of holding the flower first to her face, inhaling, and then to his. By the dozenth-or-so time he remembered that flesh-things could detect chemicals in the air, and he wondered what the experience was like.

After that he played along, and pretended to inhale, too.

By the third day he felt more comfortable around the girl, and no one else was in sight. When she talked, he spoke back. Neither could understand the other, but it made for companionable noise. When she hunted flowers, he searched for stones. They showed each other their prizes, and sometimes they traded.

On the fifth day Grand found a lovely red jasper, which he smoothed with his hands until it gleamed. It didn't serve any function, but he liked it all the same. As he played with it, catching the sun, an odd idea struck him. He could *give* it purpose. Finally, he understood the riddle of the flower garland.

Grand traded Farah the jasper for a little violet flower — not because he liked the plant, but to make a gift of the stone. A gift was its own purpose.

On their way home that day, Grand realized that the violet flower was the only one he had seen. It might have been the only one in the whole meadow. He placed it in his mouth for safekeeping.

Farah watched him and giggled. He grinned back.

Life continued in this way for another week. Grand let himself dream that the old world really was gone — the wars, the enemies, even the Master. Though brimming with energy from days of sunshine, he invented new excuses to postpone his escape.

So what if he had become a plaything? Was that any worse than a weapon?

One morning, after Grand stopped counting the days, the scavengers came home. The woman embraced them both, her smile tight and manner nervous. Farah, on the other hand, met them with kisses and unabashed glee. The old man picked her up and whirled her about.

The young scavenger displayed a string of glittering coins. His face glowed with pride. It had been a good haul.

The woman's eyes grew wide, and for a moment she forgot her unease. She kissed him on the cheek, took some coins, and left toward the market.

The old man walked over to Grand, who stood now on the floor. He eyed Farah with a frown. He asked her a sharp question, his manner stern.

Farah lowered her eyes. She nodded and gave a shy reply, pointing out the door. She took a flower from her hair and gave it to him, a token of apology.

The old man's frown cracked, hints of a smile crinkling around his eyes. He patted Farah's head and shooed her away. With the girl gone off to play, he picked up Grand and took him to the workshop.

The old man looked Grand over with a critical eye. He spoke, but Grand knew the man spoke only to himself. He unrolled a bundle of new tools onto the table.

Grand craned his neck ever so slightly, hoping to steal a glance. He saw tiny brushes, picks, chisels, and a delicate hammer.

What was the man going to do to him?

Old panic welled back up. The man would shatter him, pry out his heart. He would makc a trophy of it. He would sell it to the collector. The chisel reached for Grand's face...

...and softly tapped his cheek, the kiss of a feather. It shifted slightly and tapped again, twice more.

Then the old man brushed him off, and scuffed his cheek with a calloused thumb.

Grand held statue-still, struggling to rein in his fear, his whirling thoughts. What was the man doing? He looked again at the tools, and this time he understood.

They were sculptor's tools. He should have known. Every artifact in the room had been repaired, invested with time and care. With love. The man was a healer of machines.

The old man placed a magnifying lens over one eye, and Grand saw himself in the distorted reflection. He saw what the man was fixing.

Half of Grand's face was a shattered ruin.

The old man labored all through the day and into the evening, stopping only when the woman brought him supper. It was better fare than their usual, and a more generous portion, but the man barely touched it. He was consumed with his work.

In the glass reflection, Grand watched his new face take form. Tender, skilled hands shaped and smoothed his visage into something new — different, but beautiful in its own way.

With his cheeks scraped down until they were even, his new face could not help but look gaunt. But the old man was an artist. With a gentle cast around the eyes and a little twist of smile curling the edge of his stone lips, Grand thought his face looked kinder than before. In a way, he now resembled a human child.

He looked like Farah, if she were a boy.

The old man finished his work, curled up on his cot, and wept.

That night, the young man and his wife stayed up chatting in the kitchen — amicably, for the first time Grand had seen.

Once everyone thought her asleep, Farah crept off her pallet and tiptoed over to the workshop. She peered inside to wave goodnight to Grand, a ritual he had come to enjoy.

The girl saw him and gasped. She ran to the shelf, snatched the toy soldier, and hurried back to the workshop. She tried to press the toy into his hands; when he would not move to take it, she rested it reverently at his feet. Eyes watering, she kissed his forehead. She skipped around the room, making a circuitous route back to her bed.

The moment she lay down there came a knock at the door. It would be the man with the oily beard. Farah didn't like him, so neither did Grand.

The conversation in the kitchen ceased. The man was perplexed, the woman terrified. He rose to answer the door. She dragged at him, pleaded with him, but he shook himself free.

Before the man could reach the door, it opened on its own. In strode oily-beard, tucking a key into his pocket.

The young man's shock gave way to fury. His face turned red, then ugly purple. He pushed his wife away, and the other man laughed at him. They traded angry words.

The young man moved to strike the other, who was much bigger than him. His wife hung from his arm, shrieking.

Oily-beard didn't hesitate. He bowled the young man to the ground and began punching, punching. Blood flew from his knuckles and flecked the floor.

The woman shouted and tore her hair. The old man rose and watched from the doorway, hands shaking. But little Farah charged.

It was insanity. There was nothing the girl could do to hurt a man that size, and yet she screamed defiance and pummeled with her useless little fists. She leapt on his back, biting and clawing like a wild thing.

Oily-beard grabbed a fistful of Farah's hair and dragged her off him. He tossed her roughly, and she tumbled across the floor.

The girl climbed to her feet, heedless of her hurts, and again she charged.

This time the man was ready for her. He stopped her with a backhand that sent her sprawling. He stalked over and kicked her.

The woman screamed. Farah rolled on the ground, clutching her belly.

Grand's stony flesh tingled, his hands trembling like a human's. His crystal heart flared with an unpleasant new sensation. He had never felt it before, but he knew its name.

Rage.

Not caring if he was seen, Grand swung off the edge of the desk, dangling by one hand. He yanked the hidden drawer so hard that it broke loose. The coins tumbled past, but he snatched the crystal before it could fall.

With one arm he hurled himself back onto the desk, rolling to his feet. He brushed away tools, junk, and priceless relics, searching frantically. And then he found it.

Grand slammed the crystal into the light-drill. He wheeled around and pulled the trigger.

As the big man aimed another kick, a searing beam raked his chest, charring clothes and flesh. He looked down in wide-eyed astonishment, sank to his knees, and fell. Curling black smoke rose from the wound.

The woman and old man both rushed to Farah, cradling her protectively. The young man, nose smashed and lips split, struggled to sit up. He spat a bloody spray at the corpse.

Farah curled, whimpering, against the old man. The woman looked at him, eyebrows arched. The old man shrugged and pointed at the workshop.

The woman picked up a candle and walked cautiously to the workshop door. She held the light inside and peered around the corner.

Guiltily, Grand dropped the light-drill, drawing the woman's gaze.

She saw the toy soldier, and then she saw his face. Her knees buckled and her eyes rolled back into her head. She dropped, limp as the dead man.

They buried the corpse in the goat field, and did not speak of it again.

The next day the woman refused to look at Grand, refused to remain in the house with him. She screamed and shrieked and wailed, casting an accusing finger at him. Nothing would console her. Nothing would satisfy her, except for him to be gone.

Reluctantly, against Farah's tears and protests, the young man returned Grand to the sack in which he'd arrived. The old man frowned, but did not object. They took Grand back to the collector and sold him. They bartered eagerly and settled for a poor sum, despite the beauty of his new face.

After they left, the collector smiled to himself, pleased with his acquisition. He placed Grand in a box and sealed the lid.

Alone in the dark, Grand sulked.

Again he had failed. He had thrown away his chance at escape, risked his own survival, all to save a flesh-thing. He, who had toppled their cities, cracked the very earth to kill them by the thousands.

What had changed?

For centuries, the Master's truth had been Grand's truth. Utility was value, and the flesh-things served no function. They were as random as lichen growing on rock, with no purpose but to exist and to spread. Their rampant variation was an affront to the blessed uniformity of stone.

So why had he chosen Farah over himself?

Maybe Grand was broken, delusional. Maybe, in the Master's silence, he had finally heard his own thoughts.

Or maybe he simply preferred Farah's truths to his own.

To Farah, uniqueness wasn't error. It was beauty, something to be treasured. It was the only purple flower in a field. And though she had no Master to guide her, to give her life meaning, she still had purpose. Grand understood this now.

Like the garland, like the jasper, she was a gift – something brought into the world to make it a little brighter. A gift was its own purpose.

It was a dangerous thought, this idea of purpose without a Master, but it resonated with Grand like song to a stone. It was a thought rich with possibilities, and he had ample time to ponder them.

Grand reached into his mouth for a violet flower that had already begun to wilt. He clutched it and settled in to wait.

See Chris Cornetto's story "Heart of Stone" online at Metaphorosis.
If you liked it, leave a comment. Authors love that!

Remember to subscribe to our e-mail updates so you'll know when new stories are posted.

About the story

It's my dream to one day publish a fantasy novel. While writing one, I excavated something strange from a sand-filled well – a little golem like no other, with a spark of curiosity and the face of a child. I was instantly fascinated by him.

Who was he? How did he get there? I had to know.

So, I wrote "Heart of Stone" to find out.

A question for the author

Q: How do you generate story ideas, and how soon do you act on them?

A: I'm driven by curiosity. For twenty years, the same fantasy world has been living and growing inside my head. All my stories take place in this world, and I explore it through writing. Sometimes the exploration is literal, as in "What lurks over the next hill?" Other times it's philosophical, like "How would character X react if faced with dilemma Y?" I write stories to find out.

As for when I act on them, it's never as soon as I'd like. By day there's the job, at night there are dogs with bellies that need to be rubbed. By necessity, I let the ideas percolate for a few days, and I jot notes as they come to me. That way, when I finally make it to the coffee shop, I'm ready to spill words onto the page.

About the author

Chris Cornetto is a physics teacher by day and writer by night. In addition to physics, he has degrees in chemistry, philosophy, and psychology. He likes exploring ethical questions through fantasy settings, and enjoys long walks with small dogs.

Grow, Divide, Sacrifice, Thrive

Jo Miles

The circular driveway at the Randolph family house was already full when Chris arrived, packed tight with cars all the way out to the curb, so Chris parked on the street. It seemed fitting that there was no space left for them, and anyway, their scraped-up little Honda didn't belong next to the family's Lexuses and Teslas.

Evening bathed the neighborhood in softening shadows, drawing the eye to the lit windows of the Randolph home, which was more of a mansion than a house. Chris slumped against the steering wheel, head pillowed on their arms, and watched, delaying the awkwardness as long as possible. Grandma Patricia's silver head went past the kitchen window, bathed in warm overhead lights.

She was probably taking the bread out of the oven right now, a perfect loaf of sourdough, dark brown crust with airy, tangy insides, a recipe perfected over generations of Randolph women. Or maybe she and the cousins were cooing over Eve, the oh-so-precious family sourdough starter, which Patricia talked to and coddled and praised incessantly, as if it were a person and not a blob of yeast. Patricia loved that starter more than her own grandchildren.

Chris hadn't wanted to come tonight, but Grandma Patricia had been unbending. No one skipped the family dinner, Patricia said, not for any reason. If Great-Uncle Jerome had come downstairs for the anniversary dinner when he was on his death bed, then Chris could come, too.

The compulsion seized Chris to flee. Start the car, drive away. Keep driving, leave town, change names. Stop being a Randolph.

It was an old fantasy, but even though Chris had cut their family out of almost every aspect of their life, they'd never had the guts to sever ties entirely. Maybe it was fear that kept them coming back for anniversaries, year after year. Maybe it was foolish hope. But as long as they were a Randolph, they had to come to anniversary dinners, no matter how little they belonged.

Time to get this over with.

Inside, the house was a cheerful chaos of activity. Cousins spilled out of the sitting room, debating the political crisis in Venezuela, while a pair of four-year-olds played with Scrabble tiles on the marble floor of the foyer, spelling out six-letter words that shouldn't have been in their vocabularies yet. Chris did a round of hugs and handshakes, then headed to the kitchen.

Sure enough, Eve's jar sat open on the kitchen table, and Chris's half-sister Shannon bent over it alongside Patricia, blonde hair bobbing beside silver, whispering together like teenage girls. Tonight's loaf of sourdough was cooling on the counter, filling the kitchen with its scent, which didn't quite overpower the sharper raw yeast scent of the starter. Chris hovered in the doorway, not crossing the threshold. The kitchen had always been Grandma's temple, her sacred space, and Chris never felt welcome there.

"This is the cycle we maintain," Patricia told Shannon as she mixed flour and water with her fingers, then added the mixture lovingly to Eve's bowl. "Sacrifice, feed, grow, and then the cycle repeats, over and over. Eve sacrifices herself for our daily bread, and we feed and restore her, and together, we all thrive. Here, you try, dear."

Patricia licked a blob of smelly white goop from her finger, cleaning off her perfectly manicured carmine nails. Chris wrinkled their nose. They'd always found the fascination with the family sourdough a bit morbid: it couldn't be healthy to get that attached to something you *ate*, but no one else shared Chris's opinion – which, come to think of it, was probably why Patricia had taught Shannon and all their little cousins to bake sourdough when they were kids, but never bothered inviting Chris to join in. Shannon plunged her hands into the bacterial goop without hesitation, folding and mixing with the same entranced fondness she used to show when she was nursing her baby.

"How do you tell if the mixture is right?"

"Eve will tell you. See how she's bubbling? You're feeling satisfied, aren't you, Eve?" They both cocked their heads as if listening to the sourdough's response, a habitual family affectation that drove Chris mad, and Patricia smiled. "See? She's very pleased. She's always liked you." Shannon looked touched.

Chris cleared their throat. "Hello, Grandma. Hi, Shan."

"You're late, Christina, and what is *that*?" Patricia said.

"What's what?"

"That thing you're wearing."

"It's scrubs. I told you, I had to come straight from work. I barely got away at all — with this flu going around, we're stretched thin, and since I'm the lucky nurse with Randolph genes who never gets sick—"

"I know what scrubs are. What I don't understand is why you thought they were appropriate for a family dinner, or why the good health this family gave you should be an excuse to avoid seeing that family. If you won't have the decency to grow your hair to a respectable length, you might at least buy yourself an outfit or two that are appropriate for company."

"Sure, Grandma, I'll get a nice pantsuit for my patients to vomit on."

"I don't appreciate your tone, Christina. I left one of my dresses out for you on the bed upstairs. You can use some product, too, while you're up there. Shannon, dear, I don't suppose you could talk your sister into doing her makeup?"

Chris's lips tightened into a grimace. They'd long since given up on making the family use their pronouns. It had never seemed worth the effort, just as it wasn't worth correcting patients who gendered them female, and mostly it didn't bother them that much, just another pinprick of disrespect. Tonight, though, it was one more way to feel out of place within their own family.

"If there's one thing I've learned from running a start-up," said Shannon, shaking her head, "it's the fine line between 'wildly ambitious' and 'impossible.' You're out of luck on that one." She avoided Chris's gaze.

"When I'm gone, you'll be responsible for the respectability of the Randolph name," Patricia warned. "Christina, get moving. Dinner is in fifteen minutes."

The dress Patricia had chosen was better suited to impressing her corporate partners at a swanky party than to an over-worked non-binary nurse trying to disappear at a family dinner. Just looking at it made Chris feel thirty years older and three times as feminine. They folded their arms and stared at it, but it refused to transform into something less mortifying.

"Not really your style, huh?" Shannon asked with chagrin from the doorway. She was holding an overnight bag the way Patricia would hold a pie she was bringing to a neighbor.

"She never stops pushing." Chris's breath hitched mid-sigh. Patricia never stopped, and every time Chris thought they'd gotten numb to it, the ache of rejection would find its way in again. "She won't accept anything less than the perfect granddaughter, and I'm not that."

"It's not your fault. She cares so much about the family, about our traditions, our history... That stuff matters to her more than anything, and that's no excuse for the way she treats you, Chris, but maybe, if you tried just a little..."

"Tried? If *I* tried? How about if she tried to get to know me as I am, instead of measuring me against what she wants me to be?"

Shannon's jaw opened, then closed again. "I'm on your side. If you gave her just a little of what she wants — if you dressed up, not *that* dress, we can find something less awful — I think I could get her to take you more seriously."

"Oh yeah? Like you took my side downstairs just now?" Chris shook their head. "I'm non-binary, Shan. That's part of who I am. It's taken forever to figure it out, but I *like* who I am. I'm also a nurse, not a doctor or lawyer or CEO, and I *like* that. I like helping people. I like my life. And none of it's good enough for her."

Unspoken was the fact that Shannon had always been good enough. As a child, while Chris had hidden in the library reading science books and learning to code, their younger half-sister was the one who helped Grandma in the kitchen, who wasn't afraid to get her hands dirty with flour and butter, who took most of Mom's jewelry after she died and played with Grandma's make-up when she was way too young. Patricia had nothing but disappointment for the things Chris had failed to be.

"Chris, I'm sorry," Shannon said softly.

"I'm not wearing a damn dress. Not for her."

Shannon held out the overnight bag, a peace offering. "I know. I brought some stuff for you, old clothes of mine from before I had April. Stuff I thought you might like."

Chris took the bag and held it, like its weight could be a measure of their sister's caring. It was more consideration than Patricia had shown them. "Thanks, sis."

"You'd better hurry and change. People are going in for dinner."

The selection Shannon had brought was actually pretty decent: clean-cut and not too feminine, even a little funky. Chris chose slacks and a patterned button-up blouse that looked good over their binder. Its pattern looked like polka-dots at a distance, but up close, each dot became a cat at play. A bearable compromise between obedience and defiance. Feeling a little better, Chris went down to the dining room and took a seat next to Shannon's kid, who was delighted when Chris showed off their secret kitty-cats.

Dinner began, as always, with a recitation of everyone's recent accomplishments. It was supposed to cover the past year, but Patricia joked,

"We'd better all stick to the past quarter, or we'll starve before the meal starts."

They went around the table, starting with a list of Patricia's recent mergers and acquisitions and a reminder about her hybrid roses winning Best New Variety in the Pacific Flower Show. Shannon's tech company was on the verge of being bought out, which was a big deal, and April had been accepted at a "gifted preschool," which was apparently an even bigger deal. Shannon's dad (still part of the family in a way Chris's father never had been) was the new chair of his Senate committee. Cousin Sophia was co-starring in a drama with Tom Cruise, and critics were already talking up her role's Oscar potential. Even Cousin Darren had news: he'd come in first in the national wiffle ball championship last month.

Then it was Chris's turn.

"I gave out over two hundred flu shots this week. And one of my cancer patients finished chemo today. I was so proud of her."

Patricia made that face, the one that said, *are you really my grandchild, or did your mother adopt you?* At least she didn't say anything.

"Is it true you're studying to be a doctor, dear?" asked elderly Aunt Adelle. "That's big news."

They twisted the napkin in their lap. Where had that rumor come from? "I've never wanted to be a doctor. Nurses are the ones who get to work with the patients and really help them."

Someone coughed. Cousin Sophia swooped to the rescue, saying: "I think that's very generous, the way Chris devotes herself to that job when she could do anything she wants. We need people like her in the world, people who sacrifice for good causes."

She was trying to help. Chris forced a smile, and the spotlight moved off them to continue around the table.

When the recitation came full circle, Patricia held up a newspaper with the latest profile of the family. "I thought it was fortuitous that this article came out today." She cleared her throat and read: "'Kennedy. Carnegie. Ford. These are among the great dynasties that made this country what it is today. Yet no list of prominent families would be complete without the Randolphs. No single family has had such wide-reaching influence in fields from politics to finance, technology

to arts, as the close-knit Randolph clan.'
And tonight, my dearest family, we
celebrate another year of success with the
family member who makes it all possible,
though she rarely gets her due. Tonight,
we honor Eve!"

She folded back the cloth napkin that
covered tonight's bread, and paused to let
everyone *ooh* and *aah* before she cut in.
The crust crackled as she divided it into
even slices. The basket passed around the
table, and each of them held their slice in
their hands, waiting while Patricia gave
the blessing.

"Thank you, Eve, for the nourishment
and wisdom you give us. Thank you for
the bread that makes us healthy and
strong. You are the heart of our family,
and you always will be."

"Amen," everyone said, reverently. "We
love you, Eve!" Shannon added. Everyone
cocked their heads as if listening for a
response, then chuckled in unison. Chris
struggled not to roll their eyes.

Dinner was the sort of easy-elegant
meal Patricia had perfected so she could
show off her hostess skills: a fall vegetable
ratatouille, baby kale salad, and a gratin
starring some imported cheese with a
name that sounded made-up. It was, like

everything Patricia made, delicious. That was good, because eating gave Chris something to do while Patricia told the family story.

"Our anniversary is always worth celebrating, but this one is particularly significant. It's been one hundred and seventy-five years since we found Eve and began our family, at the height of the Gold Rush..."

Chris had heard the story thirty-two times, give or take, though it felt like far more. They poked at their food as Patricia told how Many-Times-Great-Grandmother Charlotte had helped a mysterious stranger who, as a gesture of thanks, spat in Charlotte's sourdough starter. Every anniversary dinner involved rehashing the debate over who that stranger was: a faerie, or a small god, or maybe an alien. Everyone except Chris agreed that it was something beyond human, because from that day on (the story went), the bread made from that starter had special properties, enhancing the health and prosperity of all who ate it, guiding the family's fortunes with its supernatural powers.

It was ridiculous. Not the idea that the family starter had survived since the Gold

Rush, because yeast colonies could do that, but as for magical powers... well. It made perfectly good bread — Chris nibbled a corner of theirs — but there was nothing magical about it. It certainly hadn't led to the family's prosperity as everyone seemed to think. Chris had spent a lot of time, over a lifetime of these dinners, mulling the principles of psychology that had set Charlotte Randolph's descendants on the path to prosperity, but however it started, the Randolph family success had become a self-fulfilling prophecy. The Randolphs didn't need magic sourdough to make them successful. These days, they had privilege, and that served them better than any magic.

"That's how it began. Under Eve's influence, Charlotte and her children thrived, and Eve has passed down from caretaker to caretaker, growing wiser and stronger through many of our generations, and thousands of hers — until tonight, when we continue that honorable chain to its next step."

Chris leaned forward. This wasn't part of the usual tradition.

Patricia squeezed Shannon's shoulder, beaming. "This won't surprise any of you, but Eve and I have chosen my successor. I'm not going anywhere for some time yet —"

"So don't go getting ideas, kiddo," Aunt Adelle teased.

"But starting today, I'll be training Shannon to take over as Eve's caretaker. Congratulations, sweetie."

The table erupted in applause. Patricia kissed Shannon on the cheek, and cousins swarmed her with hugs and congratulations. The aunts passed a bottle of wine around, joking about how surprised they weren't. And Chris watched their sister, basking in the warmth of the family's attention like bread in a hot oven, and twisted the napkin around their fingers until they tingled from lack of blood flow.

"And believe me, Eve could not be in better hands than with my wonderful, caring, dedicated, *brilliant* granddaughter."

Her wonderful, brilliant, caring, dedicated granddaughter. The only grandchild that mattered.

Chris shoved their chair back from the table. They didn't bother to excuse themself, because no one really cared if they were there.

Chris braced their arms on the bathroom sink, shoulders heaving as they contained the urge to scream. Or maybe cry, they weren't sure which.

Everyone had expected Patricia to name Shannon as her successor, and it wasn't like Chris wanted the job. Even if Patricia, in some hypothetical fit of dementia, had offered it to Chris, they would have turned it down. So why did this announcement make them so miserable?

The family's obsession with that sourdough starter had always aggravated them. Sure, there were some documented health benefits to sourdough, but it didn't make you smarter, or disease-proof, and it certainly didn't grant good luck. Yet the Randolphs treated the starter like a magical creature. Like a *friend*. They'd *named* it. Chris had tried to explain once, at a long-ago anniversary dinner when they'd just started nursing school and were full of new-found knowledge, how impossible it was for a yeast colony to evolve sentience. That had gotten them dismissed from the table, with a stern lecture afterward about respecting their elders, meaning Eve.

It was too cult-like for comfort. If the starter really had such amazing powers, some enterprising Randolph would have tried to analyze it, patent it, sell it. They would have gotten rich off it. That's what this family did. But instead they kept it secret, sharing it only with family members, maybe because they all knew deep down that their quasi-mystical beliefs wouldn't hold up against scientific scrutiny.

Even asking questions was forbidden. Once, as a kid, Chris had tried to put the starter under the lens of their toy microscope, and Patricia had boxed their ears for it, shouting: "Eve is a member of this family, she's not an object of study." In hindsight, she must have feared what Chris might learn.

Chris blinked at themself in the mirror. That gave them an idea.

They stuck their head out the bathroom door. It sounded like dinner was over and everyone had moved into the living room to play charades. No one had come looking for Chris to join a team, and they felt a pang at that. No one had come looking for them at all.

Better this way, though. They crept down the hallway, avoiding the living room so no one would see them, and with a deep breath, crossed the forbidden threshold into the kitchen. The room was empty except for Eve sitting on the counter. Sitting in judgment. Chris came up short, feeling like they'd been caught in the act, then shook their head in self-disgust for thinking that way. It was just a blob of bacteria with an impressive lineage.

They took the lid off, and the heady scent of yeast rose up. Familiar from childhood, yet Chris had never smelled it so strongly. Their whole life, they'd watched Patricia bake with their aunts and cousins and Shannon, patiently teaching the kids. They'd endured the family pride each time some Randolph offspring produced their first sourdough loaf. But never Chris. For a long time, Chris had waited for Patricia to invite them, half dreading what it would be like to touch the stuff, but still, waiting, watching from the outside. The invitation never came.

Well, it was their turn now. Holding their nose, they spooned a portion of the goopy stuff into a plastic container.

From the living room, a tipsy Aunt Adelle called for drink orders, and the kitchen would be her next stop. Chris grabbed the little container and snuck out the back door.

"I've got a surprise for you," Chris said. Standing at the back door of Monique's bakery, they held out the plastic container with both hands. "Can you teach me what to do with this?"

"That your family's starter? No joke?" Monique cracked the lid, and her eyes closed in dorky bliss as she took a deep whiff of the smelly goop. Monique lived for this sort of thing: even at this unnaturally early hour, she had her apron on and her dreads pulled back under a scarf, and there was already a smear of flour across her brown cheek. Unsanitary. Chris resisted the urge to wipe it off.

"How'd you get them to share?"

"It's a long story."

Chris's phone chimed twice in succession. Texts from Shannon, which was a change from Patricia and Aunt Adelle's phone calls that Chris had been ignoring all morning. *Chris, seriously, we need to talk,* Shannon said. *I get that you're upset, but the family's in crisis mode over what you did. Eve is freaking out, says it's not safe for her to be divided like this, and I've never seen her scared before and that scares ME. If you care about this family at all, please come back and fix this.*

And then, a moment later: *I'll take your side with Grandma if you bring it back.*

Chris set the phone to silent and stuffed it into their bag. Monique studied them, brow creased: she knew them well enough to tell something was wrong. "A long story from a long night," Chris amended. "If you make me some coffee, I'll tell you everything."

"You kidding? For a loaf of that famous Randolph sourdough, I'll keep you in coffee for the rest of your life."

Like a coffee magician, Monique conjured up the perfect potion for their mood, a double-strength caramel mocha latte. Chris sat on a clean section of steel countertop in the big bakery kitchen and sipped slowly while they told Monique about the family dinner and their poorly-thought-out theft. Monique worked while they talked, shaping dough into scones, sliding trays in and out of ovens, and kept gasping in indignation at the appropriate moments, making comments like "That woman!" and "Seriously?"

I have the best friends, Chris thought, clasping the warm mug between their hands. Their friends treated them better — were more *family* to them — than any of the Randolphs. That this particular friend owned a bakery, that Monique would take care of them with fancy coffee and day-old pastries, was a particularly nice bonus. And that Monique would teach them to bake bread, the way Patricia had taught Shannon when their sister was so small she needed to stand on a chair to reach the counter. Oh, how it had stung, sitting alone in the study, glaring at textbooks and trying not to hear them laughing together...

"Chris?" Monique touched their arm. "You okay?"

They didn't remember setting the coffee aside, but they were clutching the starter with both hands, body curled around the plastic container, clinging to their sense of loss no less tightly. "Sorry." They straightened up. "Family, huh?"

"Hey, I get it. You don't got to apologize."

Of course she understood. Monique had gone years without speaking to her own parents after she took Kira home to meet them and it went badly, and it had taken a long time for her to reconcile with her family. It was why their group of friends started celebrating Friendsgiving together instead of joining their biological families' holidays. That was the first time Chris had actually liked Thanksgiving.

"I got a few minutes before we open," Monique said. "Want to see what we can do with this starter of yours?"

Letting a non-Randolph bake with the family starter was the biggest *fuck you* Chris could possibly give to Patricia.

"Let's do it."

Monique laid out the ingredients like this was their own private cooking show: flour, salt, boards, bowls, measuring scoops, all ready to go. Monique filled a glass measuring cup with water, showing Chris what it felt like at the right temperature: barely warm against their skin.

"That starter been out at room temperature all night?"

"Yeah. Is that bad?"

"It's fine, but you got to feed it soon. Bacteria get hungry when they're warm, and they eat up all their fuel. You want to feed it less often, stick it in the fridge. But don't forget about it, it still needs taking care of."

"You talk as if it cares." As if it were a person. The way the Randolphs talked about it.

"It *is* alive, you know. It's got needs. This one looks nice and lively." Monique beamed down at the container full of goop, which had grown pungent and puffy. "Even bacteria need a little love."

"Tell that to my patients," Chris muttered. They had far more experience with bad bacteria than good ones. "Seriously, though, my family takes it too far. They *named* it. Patricia *talks* to it."

"What's the name?"

"Eve." Monique snorted, but Chris wasn't feeling humorous about it. "I think she cares more about this lump of bacteria than some members of our family."

That earned them a long, sidelong glance, but Monique wasn't the type to poke at a sore point. "Okay, we won't love it, then. For us, it's just an ingredient. You want to bake some bread, or what?"

Together, they measured out the flour into a big bowl, then water. "Now add about half the starter."

Chris picked up the container and jiggled it over the bowl, trying to pour out half without losing it all. The stuff was thick, gloppy. Seriously gross. Giving up, they reached for a spoon.

Monique's eyebrows shot up. "You plan on baking without getting your pretty white hands dirty?"

"As much as I can." Clean hands were important.

"Not in my kitchen. Mix it up." She pointed at the bowl. Chris brandished the spoon, and she added, exasperated, "With your *hands*, Chris."

"I can't show up at the hospital with yeast residue all over me."

"You can wash them after, yeah? You can't do this without getting on in there."

Seizing Chris's wrists, she plunged both their hands into the bowl, showing them how to work the flour and water with the existing starter until it became a uniform, sticky mass. The paleness of the dough blended in too well against Chris's light skin. They'd need to wash their hands six times at least before they felt comfortable going on shift tonight.

"Good. Now, we'll keep adding flour until it gets to the right consistency…"

Monique reached sticky handed for the flour scoop, and sprinkled more over the dough. Chris kept working it, and, okay, maybe this *was* fun, the squish of dough between their fingers. They could feel it firming up, starting to hold its shape. "It's getting closer, I think."

"Yeah, but it's not there yet." Another dusting of flour. Monique took a deep whiff, practically sticking her nose in the bowl. "Oh, that's got some flavor! I see why your family keeps it locked up."

Monique lifted a finger to her lips, but Chris pushed her hand away. "Yuck! Don't do that."

"It's just yeast and flour."

"Still gross. And unsafe, raw flour can carry salmonella and…"

"You worry too much." She drew her finger between her lips, eyes closing in exaggerated bliss. "Mmm, see? Try it! Come on, just a taste. Gotta taste what you're baking with."

Gooey fingers waved in front of their mouth, taunting them. Chris dodged, but dough smeared across their cheek. "Okay, fine!" they said, laughing. "I won't like it, though."

They scraped a fingertip between their teeth. The taste jolted them: like the family bread on overdrive. Rich like craft lager, tangy like yogurt. The taste of their childhood, so strong it could knock them over. And it was all the bacteria, the yeast in the starter. Flour and water couldn't do that alone.

Not alone. Hello! Hello! Oh, hello not alone!

Chris scrambled backward and slammed into the opposite workbench. A stack of mixing bowls clattered to the floor.

"The fuck?"

Not alone now, good, good, good. Good? ...Better. But you, who? Who who who?

It wasn't a voice in their head, exactly. More like a bombardment of words, impressions, and emotions, all mashed together: surprise, confusion, and fondness, and the sort of relief that came from the abatement of a powerful fear. Had Chris lost their mind? They pressed hands to temples, but it didn't shut out those alien thoughts.

Who? Where? Family missing, gone, gone, gone... but you, not you!

"What... What *is* that?" Monique was staring at the bowl of dough.

"You can hear it, too? Shit." It should have been a relief that the voice wasn't only in Chris's head, but if Monique heard it, that meant this was real, and that was worse.

New person. New, who? Who? New family? But... not family. Maybe family? The stream of thoughts subsided into a bubbly sort of contemplation, a fierce, hard-working churn. Chris reached for Monique's hand. *New family*, the voice decided. *Hello, new!*

"Chris, what the fuck is in my head?"

"I don't know how, but I think..." They couldn't believe these words were going to come out of their mouth. They ought to run and see their therapist right this minute, but how could they explain *this* to a therapist? "I think it's the starter. It's Eve."

Eve, yes, yes, Eve, me. You... Chris! Missing one. Always missing, but here now. Why here? Why now? The feeling of giddiness wavered, and uncertainty flooded in to replace it. Uncertainty, and loneliness. *So much family, but missing Chris. Now Chris, but missing family. Where? Why? Gone?* And, with a quiver of real fear: *Abandoned?*

"I didn't know! I took you, and I didn't know. I'm sorry." They didn't want to hurt Eve's feelings any worse. Eve's feelings! The family starter had feelings! Hysterical laughter bubbled up their throat, as irrepressible as Eve's babble. Chris's whole life, they'd believed the family was making things up, and no one never corrected them. Grandma, Mom, Shannon… they'd been experiencing this all along. But not Chris. That had to be Eve's question. Why all of them, but not Chris?

Until now.

"How do we make it stop?" Monique whispered. As if whispering would keep Eve from hearing. The starter's constant babble continued, a tickle in the back of Chris's mind.

Patricia talked about putting the starter "to sleep" in the fridge. Cold slowed down bacteria's activity, so that should put Eve into hibernation. But…

"No. Whatever is happening, I don't want to stop it." Chris had been left out of this for years. Left out — or denied it. They wouldn't let go of it now. "We're going to talk to it… her… it, and figure out what's going on."

What's going on? Eve echoed back.

"This," Monique waved her hands vaguely at the starter, "has never happened to you before?"

"I thought my family was making it up."

"So, what changed?"

"Um." It was hard to think against Eve's constant bubbling of questions, *where* and *why* and *how* all stumbling over each other. But as if the starter sensed their needs, the questions eased off. "Well, I was at dinner, feeling left out, and I stole the starter. Just part of it. I wanted to prove Patricia wrong about the starter creating our family's success." Brilliant plan, that. But more than that, if Chris was honest, they'd wanted to hurt Patricia. That much, they'd accomplished beyond all expectation.

Eve's wounded protests rang in the back of her mind: *Stole? Stole! Family-not-family, divider, alone-maker!*

"I know, I know, I'm sorry! I didn't think you were real, not the way they talked about. I figured I'd bake bread and share it with friends, to prove the family starter was nothing special. But I've never made bread before..."

Never, Eve agreed. *Never, missing one. Always near but never here. Never loved, never cared.*

"Don't be mean, it's not her fault," Monique chided the starter, then turned back to Chris. "And as soon as you did…"

"But I didn't hear anything last night when I stole it. She didn't start talking until… oh!" Chris's hand flew to their stomach. "Until we licked our fingers. Until we ingested the bacteria."

Yes! Yes, yes, yes, yes. Missing, then not missing. Late, so late, missing one, but here now, and others gone. Missing is here and once-here is missing…

"That… makes sense. As much as any of this makes sense." They were talking to a clump of yeast, after all, a clump of yeast that had apparently been the Randolph family's friend and advisor for over a century. "I've always eaten the sourdough, same as my family, but all the yeast dies in the baking process. The live bacteria must be a catalyst, becoming part of the microbiome…" Chris shook their head. "Patricia must know this."

Caretaker knows, Eve confirmed. Hot anger washed over Chris, and they couldn't tell whether it was Eve's or their own. *Missing one. Patricia hid you, hidden away, hidden away...*

"Your grandma excluded you from the family secret all these years?" Monique growled in her throat. "That's cold."

"I don't know why." Tears rose up out of nowhere to choke Chris. The only way to fight them down was by clinging to their anger. "She's never liked me. Always preferred Shannon. I always thought, it had to be something I did. I was never a good enough grandkid for her, never the granddaughter she wanted. I thought *I* failed her. But if this is true, then she's lied to me ever since I was a kid."

Shame, Patricia, shame. Unkind, unfair, unworthy.

That set Chris to sobbing. They couldn't stop. All those anniversary dinners they'd attended as the family failure, the butt of a joke, the one who didn't know the truth. The Randolphs were all perfect and successful, except for Chris.

Monique squeezed them in a hug, and even Eve's anger drew back, replaced with a gentleness that touched Chris deeply. Anger loomed somewhere behind it, but it was like (Chris imagined) a mother burying her anger to nurse skinned knees when her child got bullied on the playground. *Chris, Chris, found one. Together now, new family. No more hiding, no more hurting.*

"Because you lost your old family, right? When I divided you?"

Divided, separated, split. Eve and Not-Eve, No-Longer-Eve. Again, that wash of fear and loneliness.

"That means... there's two of them now?" Monique asked. "I guess the starter you left behind kept all the family connections, and this one's alone now."

Not alone! Chris, Monique, new family. Stay, family. Need family. Not alone, can't be alone.

"I'm sorry I did that to you. We won't leave you alone again." Chris sniffed, wiping their nose on the tissue Monique offered. "You always helped my family, didn't you?"

Helped Randolphs, liars, withholders. Chris wasn't the only one who felt betrayed by Patricia. *Now, help new family.*

Chris thought of all their patients at the hospital, some desperate, many deep in debt from bills. They thought of their co-workers pushing themselves beyond their limits to make sick people healthy again, often at the expense of their own health, while the Randolphs never got sick. Even friends like Monique, who took risks and opened their own businesses, who took care of their own chosen families. The Randolphs had everything: health, money, power, fame. They had privilege coming out their asses. Maybe the family sourdough helped make them successful, in the beginning, but they didn't need it anymore. Not the way other people did.

"If you're serious about that, Eve, I know some people — some new family — who could really use your help."

Yes! The thought surged, joyful and eager.

"Patricia won't like it though."

A pause. The next thoughts were quieter, darker, but no less certain. *Patricia, betrayer, old-family, not-family. Help new family.*

"I hoped you'd say that." Chris was beginning to form a plan.

It was mid-afternoon before Patricia found Chris: enough time for their bread dough to rise, rise again, and bake into a crisp round loaf. A bit misshapen and inexpert-looking, because Monique had made Chris do the hands-on work, but they felt oddly proud as they slathered a slice with butter and jam. The family's sourdough had always tasted good, but its tang carried a bitterness that had nothing to do with the bread itself. Now, with the starter humming in the back of their mind, it tasted delicious, pure and simple.

Chris wasn't the only one who thought so. Monique had set out samples for customers to taste. "Family Heirloom Sourdough, made from a Gold Rush starter," the chalkboard declared. "Tell us what you think!" Everyone loved it, to the point that Monique had to slap away greedy fingers trying to sneak extras.

Sharing the bread like this was a beginning. Sharing the starter itself, sharing its benefits with the people who really needed it, was going to take more consideration. Chris didn't want to repeat her family's mistakes.

Bells jangled as the door thrust open, loud enough that the regulars looked up. Patricia's gaze swept the room, taking in the shabby chic of the place, the chalkboard and basket of bread samples, and finally narrowed on Chris.

The weight of that gaze struck Chris hard, carrying generations of betrayed expectations. Oh, yes, Patricia knew exactly what Chris had done.

As Patricia picked her way across the crowded seating area, followed by Shannon, Chris closed the laptop on which they'd been researching the processes around launching clinical trials. Their plan was still evolving, and Patricia did *not* need to know about it right now.

Monique beat the Randolphs to Chris's side. "Mrs. Randolph, these seats are reserved for customers."

"I have no intention of taking space in your *quaint* little shop. I'm only here to retrieve my granddaughter and what she stole from her family."

Monique's hand found Chris's shoulder and squeezed.

"Grandma," Shannon murmured. "You said we'd talk…"

"I don't see what there is to talk about. It's obvious what she's done." Patricia narrowed her eyes at Monique. "And it's obvious she had help. Christina has never baked a thing in her life. I'll have you know, young lady, that you are participating in the theft of a family heirloom. You're hurting a great many people."

"Oh, yeah? Seems to me turnabout is fair play, considering you've —"

"It's okay, Mo." Chris patted their friend's hand. "I want to explain it to them. Is there someplace private we can talk?"

"You can use the kitchen." Monique folded her arms, fixing Patricia with a warning look. "But if I hear yelling, I'm coming back there."

Chris led them into the back, where the scent of fresh-baked sourdough hung accusingly in the air. Patricia started up again at once. "Christina, you're going to stop this nonsense and return the starter —"

"How did you find me?" Chris looked past her, to Shannon. "Did you tell her all the places I might go?" They'd invited Shannon here for coffee a few months back, and mentioned that their friend was the owner. That had been a mistake.

"Your sister was no help at all. Your Aunt Zelda had to issue a court order for your phone's GPS data. Now, I understand you may be disappointed that I've named Shannon as my heir, and if I'd known that you cared *at all* about family matters, I would have handled the announcement differently. But clearly the family does matter to you on some level, and that's why you need to return what you stole before any more damage is done." Her gaze fell to the plastic container on the counter. "Yes. I'll be taking that back…"

Chris blocked her path.

"You can have your container back, but Lilith is staying with me."

"*Lilith?*" The word came out strangled, choked by the force of realization. "You bonded with it. Didn't you?"

"You know, I always thought you were making up stories about Eve's powers. But it's all true, isn't it? 'She keeps us safe, keeps us healthy.' Do you know how many patients I have to talk out of fad diets and miracle health products that are actually making them sicker?"

"Chris, what did you do?" Shannon whispered.

"And all this time, our family had something that works! A bread that cures illness. Bread! But not just any bread. Our special, secret, family bread."

"Yes, it is our family secret, and you're betraying the family by—"

"Our family doesn't need it anymore. We haven't for a long time. I'm going to share it with people who do."

Patricia's face turned immediately, brilliantly scarlet, while Shannon went pale. "You can't. You won't."

"We can, and we will. Lilith wants to do it."

Yes, yes, yes. Grow, spread, help, help new! So want.

Patricia reached past Chris to seize the plastic container, but Chris caught it and held on. They'd been kept apart for so long, Patricia had *kept* them apart, and Chris wouldn't let her separate them again. Lilith affirmed: *Stay, Chris, new Chris, my Chris*, never mind that Patricia couldn't hear her.

"If you do this, Christina, you'll betray our entire family history. Eve was a gift, and you can't simply use her for your own ends."

"You mean like the family's used her for our own ends, for generations?"

"She's loyal to the family. I know you aren't capable of understanding that..."

Something broke inside Chris. "Why did you keep her from me?" they asked, raw and hurting. "My whole life. Everyone else bonded with her? The whole family?"

"Yes. All the blood relatives, and most of the spouses, too."

"Why not me?" Chris hugged the container to their chest. "Why, Grandma?"

Lilith echoed: *Why? Why? Why?*

"Because..."

Patricia faltered. Looked at Shannon, who stared back at her in astonishment. "Is that true? You kept her out on purpose?"

"I had to! Neither of you understand."

"So explain it," said Shannon.

"I'm trying. It was... hard. I had newly taken over as Eve's caretaker from my own mother, God rest her soul, and I felt the weight of my responsibilities. Usually, Eve bonds with spouses at the time of marriage, and with children at seven or eight, when they're old enough to understand. But you..."

Patricia shook her head. "You never fit in. Just like your father: always questioning, always a skeptic, never loyal enough to the family. I kept Eve from him, and it's lucky I did, because their marriage barely lasted past your birth. As you grew, it became clear that you were strange, too. You spent hours upon hours with that toy microscope, pretending to search for germs, and Eve obviously disgusted you. Your mother insisted that you would get over it if I introduced you to Eve properly. But I never felt sure about you. The doubts never stopped plaguing me."

Her gaze fell to Lilith's container, cradled protectively in Chris's arms. "The women of our family are Eve's caretakers. Her care has passed from generation to generation, and after your mother died so young, you were the natural successor. But you, Christina, you, you..."

Chris could guess where this was going. They let Patricia trail into awkward silence, let that silence pulse between them, before they said, "My name is Chris."

"What?"

"I go by Chris. Not Christina. I've asked you to call me that, and to use my correct pronouns, but you don't like it, so you don't do it. I assume that's what you're getting at, though. Names are symbols, and using my name would mean accepting all the ways I'm not what you want me to be." Their shoulders rose with a deep, fortifying breath, then fell again. "I was never enough for you. That's why you shut me out, isn't it? I was never enough of a *granddaughter* for you, never a good enough girl."

They didn't need Patricia's sigh to confirm the guess that they'd never put into words before. The Randolph women had a special relationship to Eve as caretakers and bread-makers, and Chris had always been in-between. Always not-quite-a-girl, not-really-a-woman, even before they'd learned words like *non-binary* and *genderqueer*. They had never fit cleanly into the family secret, and rather than try to understand and find a place for Chris, their family had left them out entirely.

"I don't know *what* you are, Christina, but you're not normal." Chris flinched, but Patricia went on unrelenting, not seeming to notice or care how those words hurt. "If you were really a Randolph, you'd have put the family first, but instead, you always did as you pleased."

"By putting the family first," Chris said through clenched teeth, "you mean hiding my true self. Pretending to be something I wasn't."

"I mean behaving appropriately as a Randolph woman! You see? You're too selfish. You would never be a fitting companion for Eve, never mind being her caretaker." She lifted her hands as if she were helpless in this, as if it hadn't been her choice. "I had to let the family believe you'd failed to bond with Eve, and it's clear now that I did the right thing. It was better than explaining it to them. Or to Eve. She wouldn't have understood."

"That's a lie!" Shannon cried. "Grandma, did you even try? Eve is listening right now and she understands just fine. Don't blame this on her, when you were the one who couldn't accept your own grandchild. Chris might be different, but they're no less a Randolph than I am. They're part of this family." She squeezed Chris's shoulder. "I'm so sorry, I swear I didn't know..."

"I believe you," Chris said softly. They straightened up slowly, facing their grandmother square on. "I don't need you to understand the name I chose, Grandma, or the way I dress, or my job, or my life, or my friends. I never needed you to understand, I just needed you to accept it. Accept that this is who I am, that this is the life that's right for me, and the life you wanted for me isn't." Their breath hitched. "I wanted you to love me anyway, but I was never enough for you. You still don't think I'm enough."

What about you? they asked Lilith silently. *Am I enough for you?*

And Lilith answered: *Human words, man woman boy girl him her them, all the same, doesn't matter. Family matters, together matters, Chris Monique together good. Enough, Chris, enough, enough, Chris is enough.*

"Of course I *loved* you. You're my grandchild," Patricia said, sniffing with more consternation than hurt.

"But not enough to let me in."

"Well, I can fix that now. Come home, Christina —"

"It's *Chris*, Grandma, for goodness sake," said Shannon.

"Chris, Christina, I don't care what name you use with your friends. Come home, and we'll figure out what to do about this new version of Eve you've created. We'll get you bonded to the real Eve like I should have done long ago, and as long as you don't challenge your sister's role as my successor, all will be well."

"No." Chris took a step back. "No, I can't do that."

"Christina." That warning tone, the one that said they were about to be sent to their room. It still unsettled them.

"You can't just erase a lifetime of mistakes and pretend it's fine. And you can't have the starter back. I didn't know what I was doing when I stole her, but she's not Eve anymore. She's separate now, her own being, her own branch of the family. That's why we named her Lilith." They couldn't help smiling over that small rebellion. "She doesn't want to be destroyed or re-absorbed or made into something else, and neither do I."

"Of course not," Shannon said, and suddenly she was at Chris's side. On their side, for the first time. "You can't just expect them to forgive you, Gran. You left them out of the *family*."

"But this new starter... Shannon, you understand the risks. It can't be allowed —"

"You're not helping," Shannon said firmly, and that was another first, the first time Chris could remember their half-sister talking back to the formidable Grandma Randolph.

Patricia blinked at her, as stunned as Chris, then threw up her hands. "Fine. I'll go, but that means it's your job to talk sense into your sister."

"Yes, we'll talk. I promise," Shannon said. And she said nothing more until

Patricia was gone, the kitchen door swinging behind her.

In the silence left behind, Chris held their breath, bracing themself against a fresh barrage of argument. What they didn't expect was laughter: heavy, humorless, relieved laughter that burst the tension in the room. Laughter that felt like the next best alternative to tears, as Chris found themself joining in, slumped against the steel countertop with one hand pressed to their face.

"Well," Shannon said, shaking her head. "That happened."

"Did you see her *face*?"

"She was this close to exploding."

Spasms of laughter stole their breath, a necessary release. "Whew! Wow." Gradually, they recovered and looked soberly at Shannon. "Thanks for taking my side back there. Go ahead and say whatever you need to say, so you can tell Patricia you tried."

Shannon shifted from one foot to the other. "What are you planning to do? With... Lilith?"

"We're still figuring that out — me, Monique, and Lilith. She's feeling awfully angry about how the family has controlled her, how we kept her for ourselves and never told her that so many other people had greater needs."

"She's picking that up from you. You always cared so much about everything."

"I've infected her with my rebellion, you mean?" They smiled. "Probably. She wants to explore the limits of what she can be. How many people she could help. She's been serving our privileged little family for too long, and she wants to do more."

Shannon took on that distant look that Chris had always believed was an affectation, and now recognized as communing with the starter. "Eve feels awful about all this. She knew there was something wrong between you and Patricia, but she never knew what Patricia did to you. Neither did I. And she..." Another pause. "She's worried about her offspring. She's never divided before, and if Lilith is cut off from the family she's known, Eve believes that could be traumatic."

Lilith's answering moan ached deep in Chris's breastbone. "Eve's right. Lilith is scared, lonely..." Had she latched onto

Chris's anger as a salve for her trauma? Probably, but not just for that. "I don't know what I'm doing, Shannon. I want to take care of her the way you're taking care of Eve. Mo is teaching me to bake bread, but there's more to being a caretaker, isn't there?"

"A lot more."

"Then teach me." Chris stumbled, surprised at themself for asking it, then slowly said it again. "Would you? Teach me, the way Patricia's teaching you?"

"Chris. Of course I would."

"Patricia won't approve."

"That's her problem. We're the new generation of caretakers, and we can decide what traditions to keep. I'm not ready to be as radical as you are, but... we've done things the same way for so many generations. It's time for some changes."

Shannon's smile kindled an answering smile in Chris, an upwelling of joy that was partly Lilith's and partly their own and Chris couldn't find the edges between them. They hugged Shannon, and the two of them stood there, holding each other.

The door swung open, and Monique peeked in.

"Didn't mean to interrupt. I saw your grandma leave, and wanted to make sure you were okay."

Chris held onto Shannon with one arm and held out the other hand to Monique. "I'm okay. I think I lost my grandmother today, maybe for good, but I got two new family members in exchange: I met Lilith, and I got my sister back. I'd call that a fair trade."

"I'm glad. Sorry about your family, though, your real family," Monique said with an apologetic glance at Shannon. "You've always had a rough time with them, and this won't help."

"My real family's right here." Chris squeezed both their hands, and Lilith echoed: *Old family, new family. Family. Here.* "Family's not about genetics. Real family is the people you choose. The people you keep in your life, whether you're related to them or not. You two are my family, and now, so is Lilith."

"Don't you go all sappy now." Monique nudged them. "Shannon, you want to stay and eat with us? Tell us what we're getting ourselves into? I'm out of sourdough, but I got two kinds of quiche, and carrot cake for dessert."

"Sure. I mean, if Chris wants..."

"Yes. Please do."

"All right then. I'd love to."

A sense of rightness filled Chris up, rich and warm as fresh bread. This was the right way to mark a beginning: today was a new anniversary for a new family, one that deserved its own dinner. That was a tradition worth keeping.

See Jo Miles's story "Grow, Divide, Sacrifice, Thrive" online at Metaphorosis.
If you liked it, leave a comment. Authors love that!
Remember to subscribe to our e-mail updates so you'll know when new stories are posted.

About the story

When I was in college, my good friend was the caretaker for a portion of her family's heirloom sourdough starter. It blew my mind that this starter had been passed down through multiple generations of her family, and I loved the idea of a living, growing family heirloom. (That you could turn it into delicious bread, even better.)

Passing down a sourdough starter isn't uncommon. There are documented cases of starters that are more than a century old, and some families claim theirs has been passed down since the Gold Rush, when miners often kept their sourdough starter in a bag around their neck so it would stay warm. There's a sort of magic in that already, and it was a small leap to imagine a sourdough starter with a mind of its own.

The story became about more than that, though: it's about hereditary privilege, about found family, and about being true to yourself. In fantasy, magic is often reserved for the privileged, forbidden to the people who need it most. It's also often limited by gender: either magic is forbidden to women, or it's a special, secret knowledge that only women can access. But what about people who aren't men or women? What about people who are both, or in-between, or neither? And why should magic only be used to help the people who already have everything they need?

Chris is an outsider in their own world in a number of ways. Their recognition of their privilege and their commitment to doing good is one of them. Their identity as a non-binary person is another, and their experience of finding their own path is drawn from aspects of my discovery of my own gender identity (though I'm grateful to have very supportive friends and family, unlike Chris's grandmother). I wanted Chris to get their own magic, and to show that while society might fuss over those artificial dividing lines, the magic itself doesn't give a damn.

A question for the author

Q: What's your favorite *non*-SFF book?

A: One non-fiction book that I read recently and enjoyed immensely is *The Hidden Life of Trees* by Peter Wohlleben, a German forester who combines his personal, life-long experience working with trees with some incredible recent science to show that trees have a lot more going on than we give them credit for.

Not only do trees change their chemistry to survive harsh conditions or scare off parasites; they also communicate and look out for each other, warning nearby trees about dangerous insects, supporting and sheltering young trees as they grow, and even sharing nutrients with sick trees. Though it waxes poetic in places, I found it an eye-opening look at such a familiar thing, and a reminder that life can be sophisticated in many ways, even if it looks very different from us humans.

About the author

Jo Miles is a non-binary author of science fiction and fantasy and is working to build a more hopeful future, both in their fiction and through their day job helping nonprofits use the internet to save the world. They live in Maryland, where they are owned by two cats.

www.jomiles.com, @josmiles

Sonata II: Shailani

L. Chan

Allegro: Shailani

This is part 2 of L. Chan's novella, *Sonata*. Part 1 ran in January 2020. What has gone before:

Sona has travelled north, up the lawless swathes of the Periphery of the Empire Sound. He's enlisted the help of Shailani, a former soldier with the Imperial Army, on her own journey to the north. After an ambush by jealous bandits from a gang Sona used to serve, Shailani learned that Sona was carrying something forbidden by the most basic of Empire law – a piece of illicit Music, far outside the reach of the Empire and its Composers. Their journey has taken them to the border of the Six Named land, country of his mother, and the composer of the heretical Music, the Lady Kristyk.

Their first greeting in the land of the Six Named was a pair of whistling arrows, tracing rainbow arcs up into the sky before the hollow bores through the arrows channelled the wind, augmenting the flight of the projectiles with Sound. They hit the earth like cannon fire, throwing dirt and divots of sparse grass yards into the air. Small craters marked their passing, the fragile wooden arrowshafts obliterated.

She could not see their attackers, and doubted that Sona could. The ground here was thirsty, the grass washed out and beaten low by strong winds. Hills and mountains in the distance, but distances were impossible to estimate across the windswept plains. No trees grew here. Shrubs and bushes, the few that there were, clung to the ground in desperation, their stems green and swollen with hoarded water. The expanse made her skin crawl, her head spin, as though she'd fall into the sky, so clear and cloudless was it.

She'd served with Six Named in the Sixty-Seventh. A taciturn people, well used to hardship. Few others who could march quite as far on half rations, function on as little sleep. They were horse folk, well used to living flesh beneath them, and so never served in the navies, whether ocean going or sky sailing, nor the armoured divisions. A Six Named would sooner sever his own legs than ride on the larger cousins of the multipede the Imperial Army deployed.

Both the Six Named land and Seribu had submitted, in their own fashions, to the Empire. The Six Named land fared better. Both countries had ceded territories and concessions to the Empire, but there was little in the Northern Steppes that the Empire coveted, the ground being hard enough to dull shovel blades, the plants mostly unscented and dry, good for neither furniture nor Empire weapons.

The complexities of treaties between countries was somewhat lost on Shailani as she brushed the dirt from the arrow's impact off her face. At least the Six Named were polite like her own folk; killing strangers was considered rude.

Sona pointed, his eyes sharper than hers after all, to a plume nearing in the distance, a border patrol. The multipede's gears wheezed under the scorching heat. Shailani made out seven riders, with recurved horsebows carved from alabaster ashwood, white as bone. When the riders came to a stop, Shailani met impassive gazes of the riders past steady arrowheads in front of taut bowstrings. Having seen the effect of whistlers on the ground, Shailani much preferred not to see their efficacy on her flesh.

"Sona of the Empire Sound and Shailani of Seribu seek passage to the Festival of Names," said Shailani, even-voiced. Seribu, Shailani mouthed to herself, the thousand. The Far Isles in Imperial common. She revelled in the use of the true name of her birthplace, rather than the soft mouthed interpretation the Empire had given it. Stay long enough in the Empire, you'd forget your places, your home. But you'd never forget your place in the Empire, no. They'd remind you; in the theft of your names, in the weaving of your sacred cloth into their tea dresses.

A ripple went through the patrol at the unfamiliar sound of Imperial Common. The lead took his horse forward, a shaggy piebald beast almost as tall as a man at the withers. He dismounted, landing lightly on his feet. Like Sona, the patrolmen of the Northern Steppes were compact, making an easier carry for their steeds – leanly muscled, worn down by sun and wind till there was nothing left but hardness, striated muscles on every visible inch.

"The Six Named have no quarrel with Empire, the Six Named have no quarrel with the Far Isles. But the Festival is for our people and our people alone." His voice was loud and sharp, well made for vast and open spaces, carrying clear across the scraggly grass and ochre dust.

"He claims his right as one of your people," said Shailani.

"Does he not speak for himself, or does the Empire not lower itself to speak to the natives?"

"He lost his words as a child. He was born of the Lady Kristyk, known to you as Lady Han. She was born of Zhi and Liao, they of the sept of the Thundering Hills." Foreign names rolled, unfamiliar in her mouth, like strange fruit. The north was particular about names, and she'd spent an hour practicing under Sona's tutelage.

"Three names are not enough, Shailani. We need Six. It is our way. If he is of our people, he knows that. What are the others?"

Shailani paused, looking towards Sona. There had been long moments between them when they'd rehearsed, when she found out who his father was. Sona nodded. "He is half Empire. His father is the Antius, Lord and Choirmaster of House Deathsinger. He was born of Typhus and Sybil, they of House Deathsinger." Those names, even more so than the foreign words, felt alien in her mouth. House Deathsinger, last she heard, before returning to Seribu with her discharge papers and pension, was ascendant, with a clear route to taking one of the Maestro positions, unheard of for a minor house, albeit one that dealt in assassinations.

Of course, the genealogies and succession of the houses didn't trickle down to the military outposts and regiments, but no son of a lord should be out in the Periphery earning his keep through banditry and accountancy. Nor should he be travelling to the edges of the known world with nothing but a retired soldier for company. Not to mention that the darkest of those with Empire blood would still be fairer than the skin betwixt her arse cheeks. Sona carried himself like a noble, but not even outdoor labour turned Empire folk his colour. Shailani had nothing against those of mixed blood. The two spirits knew there were enough bastard children of nobles in the Sixty-Seventh. But a genuine scion? Not a chance. This young man was playing a dangerous game, laying claim to names like that.

They had spoken of many things whilst the multipede juddered their behinds into giant bruises. The military, the weather, the current state of the Empire, the weather, the terrible blandness of the food, the pain of their behinds, the weather again. The young man was a closed book with a plain cover, but Shailani would have put money on one thing – he was pure Empire regardless of how much Six Named blood he had.

The leader of the border patrol sucked at his teeth. He likely had not mounted his horse this morning thinking he'd either have to refuse blood rights or let an Empire agent into the greatest annual event of the Six Named. In the end, he held out his arm towards Sona. "We will escort you to the Festival, and the leaders will decide on the strength of your claim." Sona smiled and took the leader's hand, pumping it enthusiastically twice. The leader turned to Shailani. "You too, I suppose. It would be a confusing trip otherwise." She clasped her hand around his forearm, and he hers. Shailani had learned the Six Named greeting back in the army. Sona, despite his birthright, had not. The leader nodded his head at her, a slight dip of the chin, the misplaced greeting evidently bringing him to the same conclusion about Sona. Six Named skin, Empire heart.

The Festival of Names presented itself in the distance as a sea of pennant flags, each in the colours of one of the Septs. Every art and skill the Six Named practiced was on display and held in competition. Even Music. The Six Named did not use Sound as profligately as the Empire, but its judicious application allowed skill alone to determine a person's role in a sept. Of course, the annual gathering was not without its share of feasting and celebrations. Around her,

Shailani could see the richness of the land in the people that lived off it. The Six Named were dressed in riotous colours, in the manner of a field of wildflowers. Their tools, weapons, and instruments were exquisitely made, and could have held their own against Empire craft, in utility if not in beauty.

Distance from the muggy jungles of her people pulled at her, a loose thread that would slowly unravel stitching. Truly she'd spent more time conscripted than as a resident, but barracks and quarters were no home, not with the carvings of previous occupants on bed frames, the mingling of her blood with theirs in the bloated bellies of bedbugs. The distance between her and her previous travelling companions was more urgent, more pressing. Again, Shailani revisited her decision to accompany Sona, justifying to herself what she knew to be right. They'd started out as six, charged to keep the songs of their people free. Six Keepers, five groomed from birth to be servants of their people, trained in forbidden songs, charged by their people to be a repository for their shared language — living dictionaries holding the tongues of their kinfolk, that the Sultanate was so busy erasing in its quest to unify Seribu. Not just a thousand islands, but a thousand people and a thousand languages; not easy to rule. One language, one thought — that would be easier, and the Empire was helping the Sultanate to that end. A single people gave much better tribute and trade, after all. Though her appointment had been a matter of expediency, Shailani counted herself amongst the Keepers as well. Her experience in the military helped her; she could fight, and more importantly, she had once led a battle choir. That advantage had given her a headstart on picking up the sacred songs of her people. Songs to ease the dead over to the other side, songs to welcome squalling babes into this world.

She wondered how far the four surviving Keepers were from the northern reach — the mountains where legends said that caves existed with walls of crystal so perfect that a single sound could echo there for eternity. Deep enough into those caves and it was rumoured that the Songs of Creation still echoed, the music by which the spirits had hewn the world out of nothing. Shailani had been across half the continent with the army.

She'd seen fortresses reduced to rubble by war music, watched death rain down from skyships, but not seen the scantest proof of the legends the tribe talked about. The entire thing smelled like a fool's errand to Shailani, the last ditch effort of their cornered tribe, to send five of their brightest up North with nothing more than myths and legends, and the hope that the words and songs of their people would live, even after the Sultanate took their lands and children. A bad hand to be dealt, too bad folks didn't get to sit out rounds of cards in life. She had to get back to the other Keepers, no matter what dreams the elders had sold to the girls.

Sona had his own demons to wrestle with, it seemed, drawing further back into himself the deeper they got into Six Named territory. Surrounded by those that looked like him, Shailani had figured that Sona would open up like a flower drinking the sun, quizzing his hosts about all that he had missed. Definitely more Empire than Six Named, then. The same thing had happened to her when she was discharged from the Irregulars, a stranger in her own land. Yet Shailani was only an adoptee of the Empire; Empire was a skin that she shrugged off, scraping in places, once she'd been discharged. It would be more difficult for Sona to shed.

The Festival was as colourful and loud as a marketplace, and truly it was one. Not all of the Six Named were horsefolk, it seemed. Some brought cloth dyed in pounded clamshells dredged from rivers, the weaves bluer than the cloudless sky. Others brought preserved produce and dried harvests to share, everything from fruit to dried mushrooms that brought visions and madness.

Their escort deposited them at the edge of the forest of tents that made up the festival, springing up from the dirt like mushrooms after the rain, each the light earthy brown of fresh horse leather.

"I will present your case to our council," he said, showing them to an empty tent. Shailani entered first, Sona second, leading the multipede by means of a hand crank, a soft tune forcing the many-legged chest to trot slowly after them. "Help yourselves to the clothes in the guest tent." He showed himself out. Shailani could tell from the conversation outside and the long shadows cast at the tent's doorway that she and Sona were not precisely guests.

The clothes were in the style of the Six Named, linen trousers and shirts, with buttons of knotted cloth, heavier riding jackets with cinched sleeves to fit into leather bracers for horsebows. Shailani shrugged off her headscarf and top. When she shook her clothes, dust from her journey clung to the air, sparkling as it settled. She turned to see Sona, flapping his fingers at her, wide-eyed.

What are you doing? he asked.

"Changing into something clean," she replied, keeping her face towards him to read his Fingerspeech and enjoy his discomfort. "Don't be a baby, not all peoples share your Empire's allergy to the sight of breasts, and even those luxuries are not afforded to those in the Emperor's armies. Besides, I figured you'd have peeked on the way here." She pulled on the Six Named clothes and lowered her tone. "There must be no mistrust between us, Sona. We don't have time to be squeamish. You're playing with your life and mine, just to play some illegal music."

Not just any music, my mother composed it, he said.

"So your mother was a Composer, but not in service to the Maestri?" House plots, far beyond the ken of a simple retired sergeant on a mission to save a dying language. What did Shailani care about nobles and their Composers?

My father took her to wife from the Six Named. Empire wisdom has it that only Empire blood is pure enough to wrest Symphonies from the Sound. He thought otherwise. Hidden away, she would secure House Deathsinger's rise, he said.

"House Deathsinger. Is that how you name things in the Empire, just take words and bang them together?"

You know what we do, he said.

"Kill people, yes, I gathered. Your mother wrote a piece of music. How does that help your House?"

It doesn't. She wrote this in secret. My mother knew better than to hand my father that kind of power. She only gave the House baubles. Enough to secure their ascent. Me? I was an embarrassment, not just of impure blood, but unable to speak, and so unable to join the ranks of the Deathsingers. An inconvenience to the lines of succession for my father and my sister, Sona said.

"Sister?"

From my father's second wife. There's a lot about me that you don't want to know. Power was very important to my father. He used to go on about changing the Empire stripping the Maestri of their control. In the end, I became too much of a liability for his plans: a mute, impure son of a House of singers. He torched the Western Academy to kill me. My mother died so that I could escape. If they knew I was alive, they'd tear the countryside up just to hunt me down. Sona took a breath before continuing, *Tell me what you know about Sound.*

Shailani watched the rush of Fingerspeech, almost too fast for her to understand. Confessions were a lot like water behind a levee, only emerging as a flood. She'd gamble that this was the first time he'd told anyone about it. Sona was assembling something, fingers silent but dancing, screwing, joining, and aligning a complicated series of small mechanisms from the boxes he'd always kept tucked in a corner of the multipede. When he was done, he had a complex assemblage of brass minutiae mounted on a box of ornate rosewood, topped by what appeared to be the flared mouth of a trumpet, blooming like a flower. Into this he slotted an amber cylinder before sealing the box back up.

Shailani pulled the Six Named shirt over her head, cloth buttons snapping tight. "What's there to say? Just what they teach us in basic training. The Sound exists like a drum skin or harp string beneath our world. The right tones agitate the Sound, and it pushes back on our world."

Sound is everywhere. You don't need Empire instruments or machines to use it. Look at the whistling arrows. The Empire's power is in Music and the Symphonies. More than that, the horologists created gearmusic, with gears and springs playing Music, but there's a limit to what they can do. Gearmusic is only snippets. It moves the multipede, floats airships. Nothing compared to what a choir or an orchestra can do, Sona said. My mother was of one blood, but a child of two worlds, I am the opposite. Because she was of two, she always sought to see unions, intersections. Six Named Music, Empire Music, and more besides. Any Music she could get her hands on. Horology, Sound. If Sound causes something to move, could movement cause sound instead?

Sona depressed a button on the box. It began to play the same bouncy tune that drove the multipede. Their ride began to stir, gears clanking into motion before the music eased.

A perfect replica of any Music played to it. I will take my mother's symphony back to Pendulos with this. My mother had people there, sworn to her service. They helped me complete her work, and now they will help me bring my father to justice, he said. Shailani's head spun. Sona had trapped Music in a box. The Empire worshiped no gods, but their veneration of Sound was as near religion as the Sultanate's temples and minarets, as heartfelt as Shailani's own prayers to the two spirits before her meals. The device in Sona's hands held music not beholden to the hordes of trained musicians, without the need for the massed assortment of brass and wood and animal skin that comprised an orchestra.

Shailani had a mind shaped by war, and the flow of her thoughts ran back to combat like spring rivers down channels carved into rock. What damage could they wreak, with this enslaved music? With something like this, the Empire's advantage in musicians and Composers might be nullified, the old borders reinstated. Better yet, it could be applied to Shailani's own mission, and that of her sisters. Why travel to the edge of the known world on the rumour of a legend to preserve her people's language, when the means for doing so was right before her? She shook her head, clearing her mind of the whispered temptation to slip a lintah into Sona's neck then and there, and make off with the device. Shailani weighed that against the lives of the four that Sona had bought her service with. Not now, not until her debt was discharged. Afterwards, there would be no guarantees.

"You could change the entire balance of the Empire with that," said Shailani. Sona was already disassembling his creation, returning it to component boxes. "If the Empire found it, they would be unstoppable."

They would destroy it, he said. *Sound is everywhere. Only the stranglehold of the Maestri props up the Empire. This breaks that control. The Empire will eat itself from the inside.*

"Why stop it? All Empire does is eat; and when there is nothing left in the world, it will eat itself. You're holding something that could shift the world. And all you can think about is revenge?"

Let me tell you about revenge, Far Isle woman, he said. *I'm told that when a normal person thinks, you think with your voice. It's different for someone who's never heard their own voice. If there's a voice in my head, it can only be someone else's. If it's Fingerspeech, it can only be someone else's hands. How far would you go, to avenge a loss you feel with every single thought that goes through your head? Revenge is my world now.*

Festive singing welcomed them to the Council, the singers a mix of teenage children in woven skirts, and trailing ribbons ten or more feet in length. If the song was meant to achieve anything through Sound, the effect was so minor as to be unnoticeable. The Council was more than a score strong, one representative from each of the septs. Seated in a raised dais above a cleared dust arena, they witnessed displays of skill, strength, and beauty. Those that did well brought honour to the septs, and to themselves. The best of the contestants were highly sought, their talents bartered across septs in a complicated exchange of young persons in marriage.

The dress of the Council demonstrated the distances ranged by the Six Named. The Six Named were famed for the sleek riding gear that Shailani and Sona wore. Seldom seen by the rest of the world was the looser flowing silks of those who mastered the loom, the elaborately beaded dresses of those who appeared to be scribes. There was even one, and Shailani could not help but return her gaze to him over and over, that was wearing the overcoat of the Sixty-Seventh regiment. And in the colours of a commissioned officer no less. There had never been combat this far north, so it was not a trophy. Yet there was no way there was a lieutenant amongst the Six Named. Commissions were reserved for Empire only.

"I am Qin. We have heard your claim," said the man in military dress, his facility with the Common Speech obviously rendering him the spokesman, though his tongue had the slurred accent of the north. "We have not yet heard your petition."

Shailani read Sona's Fingerspeech, translating. "Sona petitions the council to fulfil the last wish of Lady Han, to hear her music played."

"Let the boy speak for himself," said Qin.

"He does not speak," said Shailani.

Let the boy speak for himself, repeated Qin. Evidently, the overcoat was not for show; the man had seen service.

These are my Six Names, said Sona, *Lady Han, of Zhi and Liao. Lord Antius DeathSinger, of Typhus and Sybil.*

"The scion of the prodigal returns. What did the Lady Han achieve in the Empire?" asked Qin.

My mother is dead, but not gone. I have her masterwork, the union of her raw talent in Composing, sharpened by Imperial academics. A symphony, the form Empire but the soul Six Named. In her memory and as one of your people, I seek that it be played here, in the land of her birth, Sona said.

"You have yet to prove who you are, Sona of Empire," said Qin. "Skin and a story are not enough."

The Festival was host to many contests, including those of martial prowess. Oiled men and women grappled, cheered on by crowds. Others showed their skill with bows whilst riding or standing. And then there were the contests of weapons.

Shailani was surprised at Sona's decision. He seemed a planner, a tactically minded sort. Certainly he had the benefit of academy training, and growing up well fed. The one time she'd seen him fight had told her all she needed to know about his skill – he'd never fought outside of a curated match. His decision to do so now seemed like overconfidence. Shailani had seen her fair share of Empire brats with that, but she saw the look on his face when he chose his weapons and there was something else at play. Sona could have done something with music; the Six Named allowed for those contests. Yet he had chosen these two swords; Six Named weapons. The Academy would have offered lessons in arms, any weapon the Imperial Army used, but not these. The Empire man had something to prove.

Sona's choice of weapon was a pair of butterfly swords, stubby blades just over a foot in length, thin handguards and upswept quillons to protect and trap. The Empire favoured cavalry cutlasses and longer blades, and his selection was meant to cement his claim to the blood. His opponent was to be the same guardsman that had escorted Shailani and Sona to the festival, Lo, his name was, a veteran of border skirmishes and pursuit of the bandits that nipped at the heels of Six Named traders. Lo's favoured weapon was a long spear, blood red tassels dangling beneath the base of the spearhead. The contestants bowed to the council and then to each other.

Lo dropped into a stooped stance, thighs coiled to give his spear a longer lunge. Sona had one blade forward, the other drawn back; attack and counter, ready for any eventuality. Steel met steel.

Shailani had been invited next to Qin, watching with the council. "Lo tells me you spent time in the army. Sixty-Seventh?" asked Qin, and under the Six Named drawl Shailani could make out the musical twang of the low counties, southern farming stock whence the Sixty-Seventh drew the bulk of its recruits. Much of the Empire's army was replenished by conscripts, but its appetite outstripped the fecundity of its women. Its conquests, vassals, and allies stepped in to fill the gap. The Empire inevitably sent conscripts to the Sixty-Seventh, and that regiment was always on active fronts. That was the cost of Empire friendship.

"You too?"

Qin nodded. The two combatants were feeling each other out, steel kissing steel like neophytes at a dance, tentative, hesitant. Up close, the elder Six Named was more weathered than most, the dark furrows of wrinkles mixed with the lighter patchwork of faded scars. "I didn't think they gave commissions to outlanders," said Shailani. Foreplay over, the combatants got into it. Lo made up for Sona's twin blades with the reach of his spear, using darting thrusts to keep the younger man at bay.

"Field commission at Angel's Fall. General Olivia valued skill above blood, and besides, everybody else was dead." Even a decade away from service, Shailani shivered at those names. Olivia, the Steel Angel, had been the one and only woman to ever attain a general's stars, during the reign of the Regent Ophelia. Angel's Fall was the name given to her most famous defeat, a failed bid to rescue stranded Imperial forces deep in enemy territory. The authorized history Shailani had garnered from her military training explained the Steel Angel's rise as illicit; the woman herself the Emperor Regent's paramour. Regiment tradition had it otherwise, Olivia as competent a leader as the next five generals put together, the incursion part of a master plot to see her disgraced. Either way, the loss of two thirds of her men at Angel's Fall had bought her a court martial and execution. The only mercy granted by the Emperor Regent had been a soldier's death, a sword through the heart, rather than hanging or dismemberment. "And yourself?" probed Qin, forcing the conversation past Shailani's open mouthed silence.

"Sergeant. Battle choir section leader. Discharged, full colours."

The two bare chested men were glistening with sweat. No contact had been made yet. Sona was tiring more quickly, the two swords heavier than he was used to. "So, a singer. Impressive, for not just an outlander in the Sixty-Seventh, but a woman to boot, and without Ophelia's edict to protect her. Would you consider marrying into my sept? You would be a welcome addition."

Shailani snorted. "I like my boys pretty and my girls hard, but you, sir, are neither. I'm afraid that I would be of little use to a sept. Nothing issues from my womb but dust."

Qin laughed, the medals on his overcoat jingling. "There's more than that for a treasure such as you. Teaching. Train my warriors, educate my tacticians. We are a rich sept, you know. Forgive an old soldier for being forward." He turned back to the display. "Your boy fights like a man who has memorised a dictionary, but cannot string together a sentence."

"He's holding his own. You must excuse his reticence. Sona has the skills, but not the heart for killing."

"Most of the Empire have it reversed. I've seen enough," Qin said, and raised his hand to Lo. The Six Named fighter lunged, his spear extending its full eight feet to bury its point into the dust at Sona's feet, the force of the strike curving the shaft of the spear like a bow. Sona dodged the telegraphed move easily, taking two steps backwards. Lo smiled at the young man, poised to make a counterattack, and pulled the tip out of the ground, the tension in the shaft releasing all at once, sending a fistful of grit into Sona's face. The breath's space it took for the younger fighter to clear his vision was enough for him to find Lo's spearpoint at his throat.

Sounds of the Six Named orchestra tuning up filled the arena. Shailani always marvelled at the discordant tones, at odds with the polished Sound they would soon produce. Or attempt to. Six Named instruments were not the same as the Empire's. Drums they had. Their trumpets and flutes carried higher tones, with an odd vibrato missing in the flared brass of the Empire. Instead of violins, they had little drummed cylinders topped by a single finger-thin wooden stem, played similarly with a bow.

The previous two days had seen Sona mobilizing the few within the Festival with any talent at composing, feverishly coaching them to transcribe Empire script into the complex notation used by the Six Named. Musicians practiced their parts whenever they got fresh sheets of music. It was impressive to behold.

Shailani took her place next to Qin as the orchestra prepared to play. "You're helping Sona, even though he lost?" Shailani asked Qin.

"We asked for him to prove himself, not beat our warrior. A demonstration of his skill sufficed."

"He could have gone through the forms."

"Kata is to combat as masturbation is to lovemaking," said Qin.

Sona was setting up his recording device on a wooden platform in front of the orchestra, near where the Conductor would stand. Maybe they would be able to play it, maybe they wouldn't. The Six Named musicians were barely an orchestra by Empire standards, even the truncated ones that served in the army. Qin pointed at the mechanism. "What Empire devilry is that?"

Shailani stared at the elder for a while, looking for guile or subterfuge, and only found the eyes of one tired of killing. "A new form of horology, something that allows Sound to be trapped, and released at your whim." Qin absorbed the news of the world-upending mechanism without blinking, one bare foot hitched up on his chair, picking at yellowing teeth with a fingernail. "A full orchestra's sound in something no bigger than a travelling chest! You could push the Six Named borders back into the Periphery." Shailani kept her voice just above a whisper, not trusting the other elders to be as circumspect as Qin, though she'd only known him for less than a day, and the chances of anyone else speaking the Imperial Common were low.

Qin looked beyond the orchestra, beyond the grassy steppes, beyond decades of discharged service and he shook his head. "The standing army of the Empire is half again as large as all of the Six Named combined. A beast so huge that it can only sustain itself by gnawing at the rest of the world. Do you know what happened after Angel's Fall?"

She shook her head.

If it were possible, the lines on the older man's face seemed to deepen, as though the recollection tore at old scabs and drew fresh blood to skin. "Our armies were reinforced; the Capital Sound sent another two regiments to the east. History is the story of the victors, but no one won in that campaign. Stories are told by those who are alive and unashamed. After the eastern purge, there were neither." Shailani'd heard of the campaign of vengeance the Empire waged in the east after their initial defeat, the annexation of lands a full fifth of the Empire's controlled span. No treaties, no surrenders. Just slaughter and parcelling out the lands to the campaign officers, and to the Houses of the Capital.

"We in the Sixty-Seventh were at the tip of the spear, led to believe that the easterners were less than human, the architects of Angel's Fall. It was a massacre. We were blood drunk. Villages. We torched homes, farms. Women, children. Old. Young. We didn't question a thing. At least not until it was over. Sure, I had doubts. It didn't take a general's stars to tell that a couple of old men with farm tools weren't a threat. But the Sixty-Seventh were the incoming tide and I wasn't about to get in front of it. When it was over, I was an anomaly, an outlander lieutenant. I retired back home. It's taken me these decades to be able to sleep more than half the night without being woken by screams." He turned to scrutinize Sona's device. "No, Shailani, the Six Named will not stand against the Empire, not even with your heretical machine."

Sona fussed, ensuring that his clockwork machine was running, angled optimally to capture the Sound from the orchestra. The young man nodded at the Conductor. If he was excited at the fruition of his life's work, his clipped gestures did not betray it. The music started.

The similarity was faint for Shailani at first. In tone, Lady Han's symphony took after a dirge, somnambulant and with the strings and winds keening across the open plains. Drums maintained a steady pace, heartbeat slow. The players grew restless, their instruments taking on a mechanical urgency that drove their playing fingers, wrists, arms, and lungs harder and harder. Only when the piece began to pick up did Shailani recognize it, given that her own people had given her naught but the briefest exposure to it. Ninety-nine in a hundred of her people would not have recognized it, but Shailani was a Keeper; she kept the words and she kept the songs. And this was one of the songs of the dead. Somehow, it had travelled the distance of the whole known world and was being played for her by a full orchestra instead of sung reverently by Keepers.

Something else grew in the space before the orchestra, a heat shimmer, a desert mirage. The patch of bare dirt wavered, as though seen through warped glass. Panic spread amongst the musicians, faces twisting as their individual parts poured from their instruments. Shailani was not sure if they were playing the music, or the music was playing them.

When it stopped, it was the pause after thunder, the stunned silence after a breaking wave. There were tears in the orchestra, others nursing cramped arms. Qin was as shocked as the rest of the council, but military training kicked in and he was soon barking orders in the sharp tones of the Six Named language. When others had stepped in to help, he gestured at Shailani and stormed towards Sona. There was a fire in his eyes, and Shailani no longer doubted that the old man with his clumsy propositions was the same one who would, without question, kill a mother, a child, a newborn. This was a man who would do all these things, and not call it murder, so bright was the fire.

"What has the Lady Han done?" he asked.

I've not heard the piece before, said Sona, quickly withdrawing the waxed cylinder from the device and stowing it about his person. Qin surged forward, drawing a phalanx of guards behind him.

His genial features were knotted, chest heaving as though choking. Shailani circled to the side, gauging if she had enough time to get in between the guards and Sona if they attacked, wondering if she owed the man that much, or she should just let the Six Named deal with Six Named business, and get on with her own. The guards were ready to draw a variety of weapons; the Six Named favoured choice above standardization, and so there were stout axes, short swords, even a war club whose design she recognized a thousand leagues from home.

"Enough with your deception, outlander," snapped Qin. "The Lady Han left us more than two decades ago, one of our brightest. And what comes back? You think we didn't recognize our Music? The husk of it is there, but it's been twisted, just like everything the Empire touches."

My mother's transgressions are not mine, pointed out Sona. *I only came to hear it played, to see what it could do.*

"Knowing this, young Sona of the Empire, what will you do with the music?"

Our arrangement was for the music, not my plans, Sona said. He leaned in closer to Qin, even though hardly anyone in the

Six Named knew Fingerspeech. *I've been running for a long time. No longer. Now I've got something of value. Something to use against those that hurt me. Better yet, something that can rattle the foundations of the Empire itself. I know people back in the Empire. People sidelined by the order of things, who will trade me power for this; we will strike, they at the Empire and me at House Deathsinger.*

Holding the power to help millions and swearing to kill thousands. You are a little Empire unto yourself, Sona, said Qin, employing Fingerspeech again. *You're more Empire than Six Named. This nation withdraws her hospitality. You will leave the festival and Lo will escort you from our lands.*

The Festival was nothing more than a smear of colour on the horizon.

Sona, reserved at the best of times, was even more so now, the hoofbeats of the shaggy northern horses and the multipede song the only conversation the party had, in contrast to the chatter of the inbound journey. Sona had saved his mother's music, but to what end, and at what cost?

Shailani's own journey had already claimed one of the girls. She'd take her payment and leave, just as soon as they hit the border.

Shailani was alone with her thoughts, and she itched to be back with the other Keepers. To the Six Named Land and back, and she had delivered, regardless of Sona's success. Leave him to his machinations, his schemes, let the two spirits take him. She'd already shirked her responsibility to her people for too long, and no matter how skilled they were, the other Keepers didn't have Shailani's grey hairs and cautious eye. Of the four others, only Ashikin had spent time out of Seribu. If Shailani hurried, she could pick up their trail, notwithstanding that her own quest seemed even more naive than the boy's. That was her first instinct, the visceral need to protect, the soldier in her obeying an order. Instincts won fights. Shailani needed more to save her people. Like that device Sona was carrying. Force was an option, so was larceny, but both left her with an intricate contraption that she might not know how to work. She needed a little more time to learn its secrets.

"Why do you think your mother's music didn't work?"

The multipede stumbled when Sona ceased pedaling. *I don't know,* he said over his shoulder.

"I think you do. She left the symphony incomplete."

No one in the Empire can complete it. Those with the skill will not see the music, those with the music do not have the technique, Sona said.

"A child of both worlds could do it. You understand the Six Named, you have academy training. You were apprenticed to the horologists, you made your recorder. This is the Lady Han's design." This the half lie, much smoother a blend than the whole truth. Truth was bitter, lies too sweet, neither palatable on its own. Shailani had never been an assassin or a spy, but she'd seen her share of lies. She needed Sona's plans and she wasn't above perpetuating the lie Sona had been living. The other Keepers were trekking northwards, chasing a baseless legend. Shailani had never seen caves which trapped sound forever, but nestled in the multipede was a device that could. If only she could get her hands on it. No point in telling Sona she recognized his mother's symphony. Maybe even knew what it was missing. Shailani couldn't puzzle out why the Six Named and her people would share common songs when they were on opposite sides of the continent, but she stowed that conundrum with all of the other problems a soldier couldn't solve.

"You want to kill the Lord Deathsinger, don't you?" asked Shailani. Sona did not answer. "What kind of man was he?"

Aloof. Distant. Not just to me, to my sister as well. Less like a person and more like an ideal wrapped in skin. I don't think he even saw people as people, just as tools for his plans and counterplans. Even as he planned to kill me, he made sure I was educated in both Sound and war. Just in case he needed me.

The Empire had a lot in common with a barrel full of hungry rats. Those at bottom were crushed by those at the top; those at the top were either fierce or lucky and if you stuck your hand in the barrel, you were likely to lose all flesh down to the bone. The Deathsingers were the rats on top, along with the other lords and ladies of the Houses, great and small.

"Can you kill him, when the time comes?"

Sona held his hand up, fingers extended to show Fingerspeech for yes, but he balled them back into his fist and hid it.

"You'd best not hesitate," Shailani said. "He won't."

Do you hear that? asked Sona, peering into the distance.

Shailani called for Lo to hold up, dismounting to join Sona in his inspection of the horizon.

There, he said, pointing at a speck in the sky. His ears were sharper than hers, having not spent time in the military, but even Shailani could make out the tuneful refrain of an airship at this distance. Noisy beasts they were, suspended under a bladder of heated air, hulls extruding oars that terminated in canvas stretched over frames of wood, looking like the fins of a fish, paddling through the air, powered by Sound. Over the distant whine of the music bearing the ship aloft, there was something else, a high pitched whine of rapidly increasing volume.

"Cover, cover!" screamed Shailani, army instincts taking over, dragging Sona behind the multipede. The cannon shot struck the ground somewhere behind the group, kicking up divots of dirt and embedding itself deep within the ground. "Nobody move," she said, pointing at Lo's men, who'd already unslung their bows and notched whistlers. "That was just a rangefinder and a warning shot. If they wanted us dead, we'd be chunks on the ground before you notched a second arrow. Stand down. Return fire and we are all dead where we stand."

Lo came up to stand with Shailani and Sona behind the lowered multipede, using the butt of his spear to prod at a clod of dirt that had been thrown twenty feet clear of the shot's landing point. "Air navy or privateers?" he asked. Shailani shushed him. She heard the faint tones of gearmusic getting clearer the closer it got. The rhythmic mechanical cadence of notes forming the Symphony of War. Military, then. The speck had grown large enough that she could make out the sails and oars that propelled the craft through the air. They were pushing their crew hard, if they had all hands on deck instead of simply relying on the wind. She didn't recognize the flags that the ship flew.

"Military," she said. "What business does the Imperial Air Navy have with Six Named? There is no war here."

Sona held up his palm, signalling for silence.

Not military, he said. *They've finally caught me. Those are Deathsinger colours.*

The airship landed just beyond whistler range. From that distance, it appeared a brigantine, a mid-sized airship. A single windsailor emerged, wearing the padded helmet and brass goggles of the profession; gearmusic kept it aloft, the tune holding it up in the sky mingled with the clanking of mechanisms that played it. The combined effect was deafening.

"They must be confident to send just one to negotiate," said Lo.

The rangefinder shot was a warning. We are wholly within their power, said Sona.

The windsailor broke into a jog, and then a full on sprint, raising puffs of sand and dust with every footfall. Only Lo's upheld palm kept his patrol from picking up their bows. The windsailor ripped off their helmet, revealing a ruddy cheeked woman, barely twenty, if even that. Her hair was cropped short, alabaster Empire skin showing through auburn stubble.

The generous would have called her passing pretty; through most of the Empire, health was conflated with beauty, as it was wherever times were lean.

"Sona?" the windsailor asked, and Shailani detected the vocal control of one trained in the Symphony of Flow, the last of the great symphonies. A choral symphony, adherents of the Flow could use their voices as weapons or worse, with greater versatility than any single instrument. War choirs were dangerous, if limited in range; Shailani'd been in charge of one in the Irregulars. But if the sailor came alone and unarmed, then she was probably trained as a solo, a virtuoso. She'd seen a single virtuoso take down eleven enemy men-at-arms in battle; training for virtuosos was perhaps the most rigorous of all the musical disciplines. Many broke, but all cracked. Where, Shailani wondered, would the cracks in this one be?

Sona, for once, was at a loss, mouth agape and fingers silent. The woman stood taller than Sona and Shailani by far, easily able to look most men in the eye. The sailor pulled Sona in for a hug so fierce that it swept him up to the tips of his toes, but her face darkened when she let him go.

You're dead, she said to Sona, her Fingerspeech so fast that Shailani could barely keep up. *They told me you died at the Western Academy. You never contacted father. You never contacted me.*

It was dangerous, he responded. *The official story was raiders, but how did they get by the guards? They had Empire uniforms, sister. I saw them. I thought it safer for the House that I completed my training and work outside of the Capital Sound. I am done now, and have discovered something of great import to House Deathsinger,* Sona said. Shailani frowned at the lie, though neither of the pair in front of her noticed. Shailani bit her lip. She was a soldier, not a spy, and she had no idea what game Sona was playing, nor what rules he was playing by. Which was an unenviable position, considering the airship had cannons pointed at them.

Shailani, said Sona, *this is my sister, the Lady Canta. Cannie, this is Shailani of the Far Isles. She is currently my bodyguard and translator in the Six Named lands. Shailani saved my life on the Periphery.*

House Deathsinger is in your debt, Lady Shailani, said Canta.

The Imperial Army had few interactions with nobility. Was she supposed to curtsy? Salute? Canta solved the problem for her by seizing Shailani's hand in two of her own, the clasp warm and firm.

We must thank you in person back in the Capital, said Canta. Shailani half thought to refuse, to pick up the trail of the Keepers and catch up, but she looked over to Sona, who met her eye in a way that suggested that going to the Capital would be a very good idea indeed. Shailani turned to speak to Lo and the patrol. "Sona and I will take the airship. We will be safe. Your mission is complete."

"We will keep watch until your flier crosses the border, not a moment before," Lo said. He nodded at Sona. "No hard feelings about the fight?"

Sona signed to Shailani. "He said that he learned something new and is better for it," she said. The two men clasped forearms. Sona did learn fast.

Canta tossed Sona the flier helmet. *If it is dangerous for you to be known,* she said. Shailani started the multipede, the mechanical beast tinkling and clanking as it followed, while Sona and Canta walked ahead.

When they were halfway between the watching escort and the airship, Canta took a scuffed brass box the size of a child's fist from one of her multitudinous pockets. She tilted it, aligning the box to her long shadow across the wiry steppe grass. Operating a catch with her thumb, she sent mirrored flashes over to her waiting airship. Blinks came back in response, followed by a barrage of cannon fire, and then the screams of horse and man, shredded by hot flying metal.

See L. Chan's story "Sonata II: Shailani" online at Metaphorosis.
If you liked it, leave a comment. Authors love that!
Remember to subscribe to our e-mail updates so you'll know when new stories are posted.

About the story

"Sonata" is one of the longest things that I've written (and completed). I don't often work in the fantasy sandbox, I much prefer near future science fiction and contemporary fantasy. For "Sonata", what preceded the story was the world building — a magic system that fell roughly as another aspect of the physical world, and where the control of that magic ran along political and societal faultlines rather than through resource or genealogical lines. Things flowed on from there — an extant Empire with a colonialist reach, a good old fashion revenge quest and some non-traditional characters. It didn't get really steampunky until about halfway in, when I realised that the frame of having a sound based magic system would overcome a lot of the engineering limitations of steampunk without pushing the rest of the technology of the world into the industrial revolution or thereabouts. It was also important to me to retain a tight cast of characters this time round, although the roster is definitely going up if I ever return to these folks.

About the author

L. Chan hails from Singapore. He spends most of his time wrangling two dogs. His work has appeared in places like *Translunar Travellers Lounge*, *Podcastle*, and *the Dark*. He tweets occasionally @lchanwrites.

lchanwrites.wordpress.com

Copyright

Metaphorosis Publishing

Metaphorosis offers beautifully written science fiction and fantasy. Our imprints include:

Metaphorosis Magazine
plant based press
Metaphorosis Books
Driftwyrd
Vestige

Help keep Metaphorosis running at
Patreon.com/metaphorosis

See more about some of our books on the following pages.

Metaphorosis Magazine

Metaphorosis:
Best of 2019

The best science fiction and fantasy stories from *Metaphorosis* magazine's fourth year.

Metaphorosis
2019

All the stories from *Metaphorosis* magazine's fourth year. Fifty-two great SFF stories.

Metaphorosis:
Best of 2018

The best science fiction and fantasy stories from *Metaphorosis* magazine's third year.

Metaphorosis
2018

All the stories from *Metaphorosis* magazine's third year. Fifty-two great SFF stories.

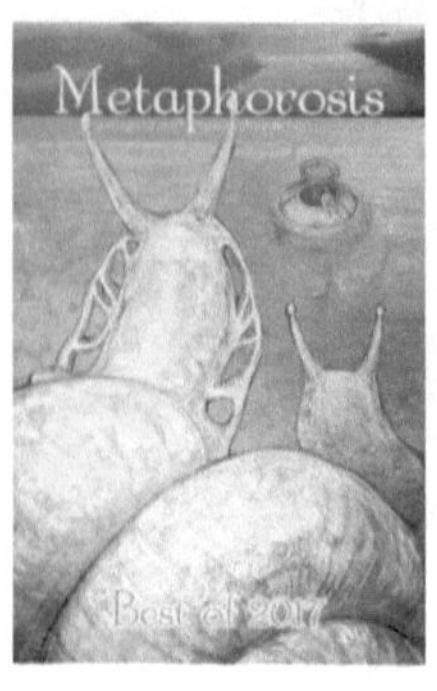 

Metaphorosis:
Best of 2017

The best science
fiction and fantasy
stories from
Metaphorosis
magazine's *second*
year.

Metaphorosis
2017

All the stories
from *Metaphorosis*
magazine's second
year. Fifty-three
great SFF stories.

Metaphorosis:
Best of 2016

The best science fiction and fantasy stories from *Metaphorosis* magazine's first year.

Metaphorosis
2016

Almost all the stories from *Metaphorosis* magazine's first year.

Plant Based Press

Vegan-friendly science fiction and fantasy, including an annual anthology of the year's best SFF stories.

Best Vegan SFF of 2019

The best vegan-friendly science fiction and fantasy stories of 2019!

Best Vegan SFF of 2018

The best vegan-friendly science fiction and fantasy stories of 2018!

Best Vegan SFF of 2017

The best vegan-friendly science fiction and fantasy stories of 2017!

Best Vegan SFF of 2016

The best vegan-friendly science fiction and fantasy stories of 2016!

Susurrus

A darkly romantic story of magic, love, and suffering.

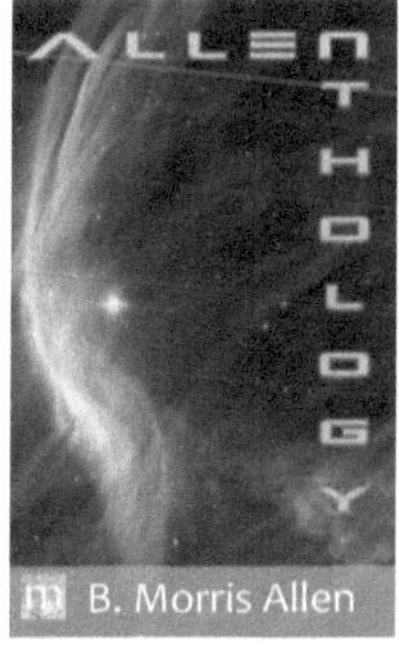

Allenthology: Volume I

A quarter century of SFF, including the full contents of the collections *Tocsin, Start with Stones,* and *Metaphorosis.*

Metaphorosis Books

Science fiction and fantasy books for writers – full of great stories, but with an additional focus on the craft of speculative fiction writing.

Score

an SFF symphony

What if stories were written like music? *Score* is an anthology of varied stories arranged to follow an emotional score from the heights of joy to the depths of despair – but always with a little hope shining through.

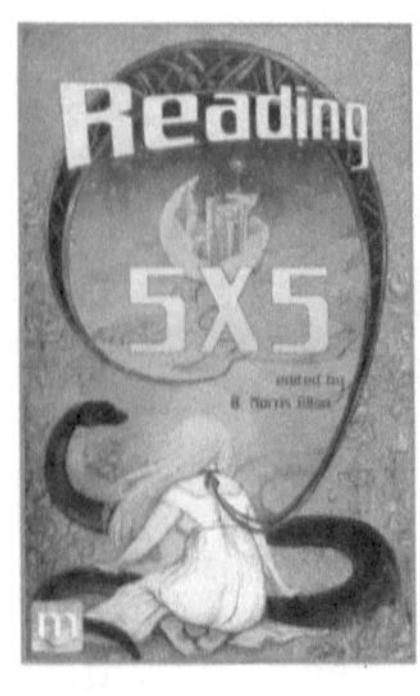 

Reading 5X5

Five stories, five times

Twenty-five SFF authors, five base stories, five versions of each – see how different writers take on the same material, with stories in contemporary and high fantasy, soft and hard SF, and a mysterious 'other' category.

Reading 5X5

Writers' Edition

All the stories from the regular, readers' edition, plus two extra stories, the story seed, and authors' notes on writing. Over 100 pages of additional material specifically aimed at writers.